April 2018

DAMBALLAH

DAMBALLAH

JOHN EDGAR WIDEMAN

VINTAGE BOOKS

A DIVISION OF RANDOM HOUSE ▪ NEW YORK

First Vintage Books Edition, October 1988

Library of Congress Cataloging-in-Publication Data
Wideman, John Edgar.
Damballah.
I. Title.
PS3573.I26D36   1988   813'.54   88-40127
ISBN 0-679-72028-6 (pbk).

Manufactured in the United States of America
10   9   8   7   6   5   4   3   2   1

TO ROBBY

Stories are letters. Letters sent to anybody or everybody. But the best kind are meant to be read by a specific somebody. When you read that kind you know you are eavesdropping. You know a real person somewhere will read the same words you are reading and the story is that person's business and you are a ghost listening in.

Remember. I think it was Geral I first heard call a watermelon a letter from home. After all these years I understand a little better what she meant. She was saying the melon is a letter addressed to us. A story for us from down home. Down Home being everywhere we've never been, the rural South, the old days, slavery, Africa. That juicy, striped message with red meat and seeds, which always looked like roaches to me, was blackness as cross and celebration, a history we could taste and chew. And it was meant for us. Addressed to us. We were meant to slit it open and take care of business.

Consider all these stories as letters from home. I never liked watermelon as a kid. I think I remember you did. You weren't afraid of becoming instant nigger, of sitting barefoot and goggle-eyed and Day-Glo black and drippy-lipped on massa's fence if you took one bit of the forbidden fruit. I was too scared to enjoy watermelon. Too self-conscious. I let people rob me of a simple pleasure. Watermelon's still tainted for me. But I know better now. I can play with the idea even if I can't get down and have a natural ball eating a real one.

Anyway . . . these stories are letters. Long overdue letters from me to you. I wish they could tear down the walls. I wish they could snatch you away from where you are.

DAMBALLAH

good serpent of the sky

■▪■▪■▪■▪■▪■▪■▪■▪■▪■▪■▪■▪■▪■▪■▪■▪■▪■▪■

"Damballah Wedo is the ancient, the venerable father; so ancient, so venerable, as of a world before the troubles began; and his children would keep him so; image of the benevolent, paternal innocence, the great father of whom one asks nothing save his blessing.... There is almost no precise communication with him, as if his wisdom were of such major cosmic scope and of such grand innocence that it could not perceive the minor anxieties of his human progeny, nor be transmuted to the petty precision of human speech.

"Yet it is this very detachment which comforts, and which is evidence, once more, of some original and primal vigor that has somehow remained inaccessible to whatever history, whatever immediacy might diminish it. Damballah's very presence, like the simple, even absent-minded caress of a father's hand, brings peace.... Damballah is himself unchanged by life, and so is at once the ancient past and the assurance of the future....

"Associated with Damballah as members of the Sky Pantheon, are Badessy, the wind, Sobo and Agarou Tonerre, the thunder.... They seem to belong to another period of history. Yet precisely because these divinities are, to a certain extent, vestigial, they give, like Damballah's detachment, a sense of historical extension, of the ancient origin of the race. To invoke them today is to stretch one's hand back to that time and to gather up all history into a solid, contemporary ground beneath one's feet."

One song invoking Damballah requests that he "Gather up the Family."

Quotation and citation from
Maya Deren's *Divine Horsemen:
The Voodoo Gods of Haiti.*

A BEGAT CHART

████████████████████████████████

1860s   Sybela and Charlie arrive in Pittsburgh; bring two children with them; eighteen more born in next twenty-five years.

1880s   Maggie Owens, oldest daughter of Sybela and Charlie, marries Buck Hollinger; bears nine children among whom are four girls—Aida, Gertrude, Gaybrella, Bess.

1900s   Hollinger girls marry—Aida to Bill Campbell; Gaybrella to Joe Hardin (three children: Fauntleroy, Ferdinand, Hazel); Bess to Riley Simpkins (one son: Eugene)—except Gert, who bears her children out of wedlock. Aida and Bill Campbell raise Gert's daughter, Freeda.

1920s   Freeda Hollinger marries John French; bears four children who survive: Lizabeth, Geraldine, Carl and Martha.

1940s   Lizabeth French marries Edgar Lawson; bears five children among whom are John, Shirley and Thomas.

1960s   Lizabeth's children begin to marry, propagate—not always in that order. John marries Judy and produces two sons (Jake and Dan); Shirley marries Rashad and bears three daughters (Keesha, Tammy, and Kaleesha); Tommy marries Sarah and produces one son (Clyde); etc. . . .

CONTENTS

FAMILY TREE

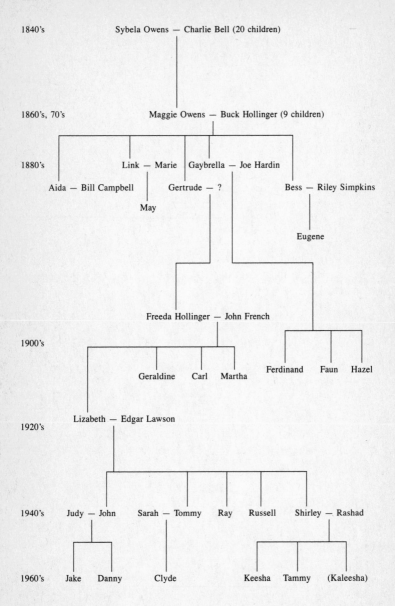

DAMBALLAH

ORION let the dead, gray cloth slide down his legs and stepped into the river. He picked his way over slippery stones till he stood calf deep. Dropping to one knee he splashed his groin, then scooped river to his chest, both hands scrubbing with quick, kneading spirals. When he stood again, he stared at the distant gray clouds. A hint of rain in the chill morning air, a faint, clean presence rising from the far side of the hills. The promise of rain coming to him as all things seemed to come these past few months, not through eyes or ears or nose but entering his black skin as if each pore had learned to feel and speak.

He watched the clear water race and ripple and pucker. Where the sun cut through the pine trees and slanted into the water he could see the bottom, see black stones, speckled stones, shining stones whose light came from within. Above a stump at the far edge of the river, clouds of insects hovered. The water was darker there, slower, appeared to stand in deep pools where tangles of root, bush and weed hung over the bank. Orion thought of the eldest priest chalking a design on the floor of the sacred *obi*. Drawing the watery door no living hands

could push open, the crossroads where the spirits passed between worlds. His skin was becoming like that in-between
place the priest scratched in the dust. When he walked the cane
rows and dirt paths of the plantation he could feel the air of
this strange land wearing out his skin, rubbing it thinner and
thinner until one day his skin would not be thick enough to
separate what was inside from everything outside. Some days
his skin whispered he was dying. But he was not afraid. The
voices and faces of his fathers bursting through would not
drown him. They would sweep him away, carry him home
again.

In his village across the sea were men who hunted and fished
with their voices. Men who could talk the fish up from their
shadowy dwellings and into the woven baskets slung over the
fishermen's shoulders. Orion knew the fish in this cold river
had forgotten him, that they were darting in and out of his legs.
If the whites had not stolen him, he would have learned the
fishing magic. The proper words, the proper tones to please
the fish. But here in this blood-soaked land everything was
different. Though he felt their slick bodies and saw the sudden
dimples in the water where they were feeding, he understood
that he would never speak the language of these fish. No more
than he would ever speak again the words of the white people
who had decided to kill him.

The boy was there again hiding behind the trees. He could
be the one. This boy born so far from home. This boy who
knew nothing but what the whites told him. This boy could
learn the story and tell it again. Time was short but he could
be the one.

"That Ryan, he a crazy nigger. One them wild African
niggers act like he fresh off the boat. Kind you stay away from
less you lookin for trouble." Aunt Lissy had stopped popping
string beans and frowned into the boy's face. The pause in the
steady drumming of beans into the iron pot, the way she
scrunched up her face to look mean like one of the Master's
pit bulls told him she had finished speaking on the subject and
wished to hear no more about it from him. When the long green
pods began to shuttle through her fingers again, it sounded like
she was cracking her knuckles, and he expected something
black to drop into the huge pot.

"Fixin to rain good. Heard them frogs last night just a singing at the clouds. Frog and all his brothers calling down the thunder. Don't rain soon them fields dry up and blow away." The boy thought of the men trudging each morning to the fields. Some were brown, some yellow, some had red in their skins and some white as the Master. Ryan black, but Aunt Lissy blacker. Fat, shiny blue-black like a crow's wing.

"Sure nuff crazy." Old woman always talking. Talking and telling silly stories. The boy wanted to hear something besides an old woman's mouth. He had heard about frogs and bears and rabbits too many times. He was almost grown now, almost ready to leave in the mornings with the men. What would they talk about? Would Orion's voice be like the hollers the boy heard early in the mornings when the men still sleepy and the sky still dark and you couldn't really see nobody but knew they were there when them cries and hollers came rising through the mist.

Pine needles crackled with each step he took, and the boy knew old Ryan knew somebody spying on him. Old nigger guess who it was, too. But if Ryan knew, Ryan didn't care. Just waded out in that water like he the only man in the world. Like maybe wasn't no world. Just him and that quiet place in the middle of the river. Must be fishing out there, some funny old African kind of fishing. Nobody never saw him touch victuals Master set out and he had to be eating something, even if he was half crazy, so the nigger must be fishing for his breakfast. Standing there like a stick in the water till the fish forgot him and he could snatch one from the water with his beaky fingers.

A skinny-legged, black waterbird in the purring river. The boy stopped chewing his stick of cane, let the sweet juice blend with his spit, a warm syrup then whose taste he prolonged by not swallowing, but letting it coat his tongue and the insides of his mouth, waiting patiently like the figure in the water waited, as the sweet taste seeped away. All the cane juice had trickled down his throat before he saw Orion move. After the stillness, the illusion that the man was a tree rooted in the rocks at the riverbed, when motion came, it was too swift to follow. Not so much a matter of seeing Orion move as it was feeling the man's eyes inside him, hooking him before he could crouch

19

lower in the weeds. Orion's eyes on him and through him boring a hole in his chest and thrusting into that space one word *Damballah*. Then the hooded eyes were gone.

On a spoon you see the shape of a face is an egg. Or two eggs because you can change the shape from long oval to moons pinched together at the middle seam or any shape egg if you tilt and push the spoon closer or farther away. Nothing to think about. You go with Mistress to the chest in the root cellar. She guides you with a candle and you make a pouch of soft cloth and carefully lay in each spoon and careful it don't jangle as up and out of the darkness following her rustling dresses and petticoats up the earthen steps each one topped by a plank which squirms as you mount it. You are following the taper she holds and the strange smell she trails and leaves in rooms. Then shut up in a room all day with nothing to think about. With rags and pieces of silver. Slowly you rub away the tarnished spots; it is like finding something which surprises you though you knew all the time it was there. Spoons lying on the strip of indigo: perfect, gleaming fish you have coaxed from the black water.

Damballah was the word. Said it to Aunt Lissy and she went upside his head, harder than she had ever slapped him. Felt like crumpling right there in the dust of the yard it hurt so bad but he bit his lip and didn't cry out, held his ground and said the word again and again silently to himself, pretending nothing but a bug on his burning cheek and twitched and sent it flying. Damballah. Be strong as he needed to be. Nothing touch him if he don't want. Before long they'd cut him from the herd of pickaninnies. No more chasing flies from the table, no more silver spoons to get shiny, no fat, old woman telling him what to do. He'd go to the fields each morning with the men. Holler like they did before the sun rose to burn off the mist. Work like they did from can to caint. From first crack of light to dusk when the puddles of shadow deepened and spread so you couldn't see your hands or feet or the sharp tools hacking at the cane.

He was already taller than the others, a stork among the chicks scurrying behind Aunt Lissy. Soon he'd rise with the conch horn and do a man's share so he had let the fire rage on half his face and thought of the nothing always there to think of. In the spoon, his face long and thin as a finger. He looked for the print of Lissy's black hand on his cheek, but the image would not stay still. Dancing like his face reflected in the river. Damballah. "Don't you ever, you hear me, ever let me hear that heathen talk no more. You hear me, boy? You talk Merican, boy." Lissy's voice like chicken cackle. And his head a barn packed with animal noise and animal smell. His own head but he had to sneak round in it. Too many others crowded in there with him. His head so crowded and noisy lots of time don't hear his own voice with all them braying and cackling.

Orion squatted the way the boy had seen the other old men collapse on their haunches and go still as a stump. Their bony knees poking up and their backsides resting on their ankles. Looked like they could sit that way all day, legs folded under them like wings. Orion drew a cross in the dust. Damballah. When Orion passed his hands over the cross the air seemed to shimmer like it does above a flame or like it does when the sun so hot you can see waves of heat rising off the fields. Orion talked to the emptiness he shaped with his long black fingers. His eyes were closed. Orion wasn't speaking but sounds came from inside him the boy had never heard before, strange words, clicks, whistles and grunts. A singsong moan that rose and fell and floated like the old man's busy hands above the cross. Damballah like a drum beat in the chant. Damballah a place the boy could enter, a familiar sound he began to anticipate, a sound outside of him which slowly forced its way inside, a sound measuring his heartbeat then one with the pumping surge of his blood.

The boy heard part of what Lissy saying to Primus in the cooking shed: "Ryan he yell that heathen word right in the middle of Jim talking bout Sweet Jesus the Son of God. Jump up like he snake bit and scream that word so everybody hushed, even the white folks what came to hear Jim preach. Simple Ryan standing there at the back of the chapel like a knot poked out on somebody's forehead. Lookin like a nigger caught wid his hand in the chicken coop. Screeching like some crazy hoot owl while Preacher Jim praying the word of the Lord. They gon kill that simple nigger one day."

Dear Sir:
   The nigger Orion which I purchased of you in good

21

faith sight unseen on your promise that he was of sound constitution "a full grown and able-bodied house servant who can read, write, do sums and cipher" to recite the exact words of your letter dated April 17, 1852, has proved to be a burden, a deficit to the economy of my plantation rather than the asset I fully believed I was receiving when I agreed to pay the price you asked. Of the vaunted intelligence so rare in his kind, I have seen nothing. Not an English word has passed through his mouth since he arrived. Of his docility and tractability I have seen only the willingness with which he bares his leatherish back to receive the stripes constant misconduct earn him. He is a creature whose brutish habits would shame me were he quartered in my kennels. I find it odd that I should write at such length about any nigger, but seldom have I been so struck by the disparity between promise and performance. As I have accrued nothing but expense and inconvenience as a result of his presence, I think it only just that you return the full amount I paid for this flawed *piece of the Indies*.

You know me as an honest and fair man and my regard for those same qualities in you prompts me to write this letter. I am not a harsh master, I concern myself with the spiritual as well as the temporal needs of my slaves. My nigger Jim is renowned in this county as a preacher. Many say I am foolish, that the words of scripture are wasted on these savage blacks. I fear you have sent me a living argument to support the critics of my Christianizing project. Among other absences of truly human qualities I have observed in this Orion is the utter lack of a soul.

She said it time for Orion to die. Broke half the overseer's bones knocking him off his horse this morning and everybody thought Ryan done run away sure but Mistress come upon the crazy nigger at suppertime on the big house porch naked as the day he born and he just sat there staring into her eyes till Mistress screamed and run away. Aunt Lissy said Ryan ain't studying no women, ain't gone near to woman since he been here and she say his ain't the first black butt Mistress done seen all them nearly grown boys walkin round summer in the

22

onliest shirt Master give em barely come down to they knees and niggers man nor woman don't get drawers the first. Mistress and Master both seen plenty. Wasn't what she saw scared her less she see the ghost leaving out Ryan's body.

The ghost wouldn't steam out the top of Orion's head. The boy remembered the sweaty men come in from the fields at dusk when the nights start to cool early, remembered them with the drinking gourds in they hands scooping up water from the wooden barrel he filled, how they throw they heads back and the water trickles from the sides of they mouth and down they chin and they let it roll on down they chests, and the smoky steam curling off they shoulders. Orion's spirit would not rise up like that but wiggle out his skin and swim off up the river.

The boy knew many kinds of ghosts and learned the ways you get round their tricks. Some spirits almost good company and he filled the nothing with jingles and whistles and took roundabout paths and sang to them when he walked up on a crossroads and yoo-hooed at doors. No way you fool the haunts if a spell conjured strong on you, no way to miss a beating if it your day to get beat, but the ghosts had everything in they hands, even the white folks in they hands. You know they there, you know they floating up in the air watching and counting and remembering them strokes Ole Master laying cross your back.

They dragged Orion across the yard. He didn't buck or kick but it seemed as if the four men carrying him were struggling with a giant stone rather than a black bag of bones. His ashy nigger weight swung between the two pairs of white men like a lazy hammock but the faces of the men all red and twisted. They huffed and puffed and sweated through they clothes carrying Ryan's bones to the barn. The dry spell had layered the yard with a coat of dust. Little squalls of yellow spurted from under the men's boots. Trudging steps heavy as if each man carried seven Orions on his shoulders. Four grown men struggling with one string of black flesh. The boy had never seen so many white folks dealing with one nigger. Aunt Lissy had said it time to die and the boy wondered what Ryan's ghost would think dropping onto the dust surrounded by the scowling faces of the Master and his overseers.

One scream that night. Like a bull when they cut off his

maleness. Couldn't tell who it was. A bull screaming once that
night and torches burning in the barn and Master and the men
coming out and no Ryan.

Mistress crying behind a locked door and Master messing
with Patty down the quarters.

In the morning light the barn swelling and rising and tee-
tering in the yellow dust, moving the way you could catch the
ghost of something in a spoon and play with it, bending it,
twisting it. That goldish ash on everybody's bare shins. Nobody
talking. No cries nor hollers from the fields. The boy watched
till his eyes hurt, waiting for a moment when he could slip
unseen into the shivering barn. On his hands and knees hiding
under a wagon, then edging sideways through the loose boards
and wedge of space where the weathered door hung crooked
on its hinge.

The interior of the barn lay in shadows. Once beyond the
sliver of light coming in at the cracked door the boy stood still
till his eyes adjusted to the darkness. First he could pick out
the stacks of hay, the rough partitions dividing the animals.
The smells, the choking heat there like always, but rising above
these familiar sensations the buzz of flies, unnaturally loud,
as if the barn breathing and each breath shook the wooden
walls. Then the boy's eyes followed the sound to an open space
at the center of the far wall. A black shape there. Orion there,
floating in his own blood. The boy ran at the blanket of flies.
When he stomped, some of the flies buzzed up from the carcass.
Others too drunk on the shimmering blood ignored him except
to join the ones hovering above the body in a sudden droning
peal of annoyance. He could keep the flies stirring but they
always returned from the recesses of the high ceiling, the dark
corners of the building, to gather in a cloud above the body.
The boy looked for something to throw. Heard his breath,
heavy and threatening like the sound of the flies. He sank to
the dirt floor, sitting cross-legged where he had stood. He
moved only once, ten slow paces away from Orion and back
again, near enough to be sure, to see again how the head had
been cleaved from the rest of the body, to see how the ax and
tongs, branding iron and other tools were scattered around the
corpse, to see how one man's hat and another's shirt, a letter

that must have come from someone's pocket lay about in a helter-skelter way as if the men had suddenly bolted before they had finished with Orion.

Forgive him, Father. I tried to the end of my patience to restore his lost soul. I made a mighty effort to bring him to the Ark of Salvation but he had walked in darkness too long. He mocked Your Grace. He denied Your Word. Have mercy on him and forgive his heathen ways as you forgive the soulless beasts of the fields and birds of the air.

She say Master still down slave row. She say everybody fraid to go down and get him. Everybody fraid to open the barn door. Overseer half dead and the Mistress still crying in her locked room and that barn starting to stink already with crazy Ryan and nobody gon get him.

And the boy knew his legs were moving and he knew they would carry him where they needed to go and he knew the legs belonged to him but he could not feel them, he had been sitting too long thinking on nothing for too long and he felt the sweat running on his body but his mind off somewhere cool and quiet and hard and he knew the space between his body and mind could not be crossed by anything, knew you mize well try to stick the head back on Ryan as try to cross that space. So he took what he needed out of the barn, unfolding, getting his gangly crane's legs together under him and shouldered open the creaking double doors and walked through the flame in the center where he had to go.

Damballah said it be a long way a ghost be going and Jordan chilly and wide and a new ghost take his time getting his wings together. Long way to go so you can sit and listen till the ghost ready to go on home. The boy wiped his wet hands on his knees and drew the cross and said the word and settled down and listened to Orion tell the stories again. Orion talked and he listened and couldn't stop listening till he saw Orion's eyes rise up through the back of the severed skull and lips rise up through the skull and the wings of the ghost measure out the rhythm of one last word.

Late afternoon and the river slept dark at its edges like it did in the mornings. The boy threw the head as far as he could and he knew the fish would hear it and swim to it and welcome it. He knew they had been waiting. He knew the ripples would touch him when he entered.

DADDY GARBAGE

"Be not dismayed
What ere betides..."

DADDY GARBAGE was a dog. Lemuel Strayhorn whose iceball cart is always right around the corner on Hamilton just down from Homewood Avenue is the one who named the dog and since he named him, claimed him, and Daddy Garbage must have agreed because he sat on the sidewalk beside Lemuel Strayhorn or slept in the shade under the two-wheeled cart or when it got too cold for iceballs, followed Strayhorn through the alleys on whatever errands and hustles the man found during the winter to keep food on the stove and smoke in the chimney of the little shack behind Dumferline. The dog was long dead but Lemuel Strayhorn still peddled the paper cups of crushed ice topped with sweet syrup, and he laughed and said, "Course I remember that crazy animal. Sure I do. And named him Daddy Garbage alright, but can't say now why I did. Must have had a reason though. Must been a good reason at the time. And you a French, ain't you? One of John French's girls. See him plain as day in your face, gal. Which one is you? Lemme see now. There was Lizabeth, the oldest, and Geraldine and one more . . ."

She answers: "Geraldine, Mr. Strayhorn."

"Sure you are. That's right. And you done brought all these beautiful babies for some ices."

"You still make the best."

"Course I do. Been on this corner before you was born. Knew your daddy when he first come to Homewood."

"This is his grandson, Lizabeth's oldest, John. And those two boys are his children. The girls belong to Lizabeth's daughter, Shirley."

"You got fine sons there, and them pretty little girls, too. Can hear John French now, braggin bout his children. He should be here today. You all want ices? You want big or small?"

"Small for the kids and I want a little one, please, and he'll take a big one, I know."

"You babies step up and tell me what kind you want. Cherry, lemon, grape, orange and tutti-frutti. Got them all."

"You remember Mr. Strayhorn. Don't you, John?"

"Uh huh. I think I remember Daddy Garbage too."

"You might of seen a dog around, son, but wasn't no Daddy Garbage. Naw, you way too young."

"Mr. Strayhorn had Daddy Garbage when I was a little girl. A big, rangy, brown dog. Looked like a wolf. Scare you half to death if you didn't know he was tame and never bothered anybody."

"Didn't bother nobody long as they didn't bother him. But that was one fighting dog once he got started. Dogs got so they wouldn't even bark when Daddy Garbage went by. Tore up some behinds in his day, yes, he did."

"Wish you could remember how he got that name."

"Wish I could tell you, too. But it's a long time ago. Some things I members plain as day, but you mize well be talking to a light post you ask me bout others. Shucks, Miss French. Been on this corner making iceballs, seem like four hundred years if it's a day."

"You don't get any older. And I bet you still remember what you want to remember. You look fine to me, Mr. Strayhorn. Look like you might be here another four hundred at least."

"Maybe I will. Yes mam, just might. You children eat them ices up now and don't get none on them nice clothes and God bless you all."

"I'm going to ask you about that name again."

"Just might remember next time. You ask me again."

"I surely will. . . ."

Snow fell all night and in the morning Homewood seemed smaller. Whiteness softened the edges of things, smoothed out the spaces between near and far. Trees drooped, the ground rose up a little higher, the snow glare in your eyes discouraged a long view, made you attentive to what was close at hand, what was familiar, yet altered and harmonized by the blanket of whiteness. The world seemed smaller till you got out in it and understood that the glaze which made the snow so lustrous had been frozen there by the wind, and sudden gusts would sprinkle your face with freezing particles from the drifts as you leaned forward to get a little closer to the place you wanted to go, the place which from your window as you surveyed the new morning and the untouched snow seemed closer than it usually was.

The only way to make it up the alley behind Dumferline was to stomp right into the drifted snow as if the worn shoes on your feet and the pants legs pegged and tucked into the tops of your socks really kept out the snow. Strayhorn looked behind him at the holes he had punched in the snow. Didn't seem like he had been zigzagging that much. Looked like the tracks of somebody been pulling on a jug of Dago Red already this morning. The dog's trail wandered even more than his, a nervous tributary crossing and recrossing its source. Dog didn't seem to mind the snow or the cold, sometimes even seemed fool enough to like it, rolling on his side and kicking up his paws or bounding to a full head of steam then leaping and belly flopping splay-legged in a shower of white spray. Still a lot of pup in the big animal. Some dogs never lost those ways. With this one, this garbage-can-raiding champion he called Daddy Garbage, Strayhorn knew it was less holding on to puppy ways than it was stone craziness, craziness age nor nothing else ever going to change.

Strayhorn lifts his foot and smacks off the snow. Balances a second on one leg but can't figure anything better to do with his clean foot so plunges it again into the snow. Waste of time brushing them off. Going to be a cold, nasty day and nothing for it. Feet get numb and gone soon anyway. Gone till he can

31

toast them in front of a fire. He steps through the crust again and the crunch of his foot breaks a stillness older than the man, the alley, the city growing on steep hills.

Somebody had set a lid of peeling wood atop a tin can. Daddy Garbage was up on his hind legs, pushing with his paws and nose against the snow-capped cover. The perfect symmetry of the crown of snow was the first to go, gouged by the dog's long, worrying snout. Next went the can. Then the lean-backed mongrel sprawled over the metal drum, mounting it and getting away from it simultaneously so he looked like a clumsy seal trying to balance on a ball. Nothing new to Strayhorn. The usual ungodly crash was muffled by the snow but the dog's nails scraped as loudly as they always did against garbage cans. The spill looked clean and bright against the snow, catching Strayhorn's eye for a moment, but a glance was all he would spare because he knew the trifling people living in those shacks behind Dumferline didn't throw nothing away unless it really was good for nothing but garbage. Slim pickins sure enough, and he grunted over his shoulder at the dog to quit fooling and catch up.

When he looked back again, back at his solitary track, at the snow swirls whipped up by the wind, at the thick rug of snow between the row houses, at the whiteness clinging to window ledges and doorsills and ragtag pieces of fence, back at the overturned barrel and the mess spread over the snow, he saw the dog had ignored him and stood stiff-legged, whining at a box disgorged from the can.

He cursed the dog and whistled him away from whatever foolishness he was prying into. Nigger garbage ain't worth shit, Strayhorn muttered, half to the dog, half to the bleakness and the squalor of the shanties disguised this bright morning by snowfall. What's he whining about and why am I going back to see. Mize well ask a fool why he's a fool as do half the things I do.

To go back down the alley meant walking into the wind. Wind cutting steady in his face and the cross drafts snapping between the row houses. He would snatch that dog's eyeballs loose. He would teach it to come when he called whether or not some dead rat or dead cat stuffed up in a box got his nose open.

"Daddy Garbage, I'm gonna have a piece of your skull."

But the dog was too quick and Strayhorn's swipe disturbed nothing but the frigid air where the scruff of the dog's neck had been. Strayhorn tried to kick away the box. If he hadn't been smacking at the dog and the snow hadn't tricked his legs, he would have sent it flying, but his foot only rolled the box over.

At first Strayhorn thought it was a doll. A little dark brown doll knocked from the box. A worn out babydoll like he'd find sometimes in people's garbage too broken up to play with anymore. A little, battered, brown-skinned doll. But when he looked closer and stepped away, and then shuffled nearer again, whining, stiff-legged like the dog, he knew it was something dead.

"Aw shit, aw shit, Daddy Garbage." When he knelt, he could hear the dog panting beside him, see the hot, rank steam, and smell the wet fur. The body lay face down in the snow, only its head and shoulders free of the newspapers stuffed in the box. Some of the wadded paper had blown free and the wind sent it scudding across the frozen crust of snow.

The child was dead and the man couldn't touch it and he couldn't leave it alone. Daddy Garbage had sidled closer. This time the swift, vicious blow caught him across the skull. The dog retreated, kicking up a flurry of snow, snarling, clicking his teeth once before he began whimpering from a distance. Under his army greatcoat Strayhorn wore the gray wool hunting vest John French had given him after John French won all that money and bought himself a new leather one with brass snaps. Strayhorn draped his overcoat across the upright can the dog had ignored, unpinned the buttonless vest from his chest and spread it on the snow. A chill was inside him. Nothing in the weather could touch him now. Strayhorn inched forward on his knees till his shadow fell across the box. He was telling his hands what they ought to do, but they were sassing. He cursed his raggedy gloves, the numb fingers inside them that would not do his bidding.

The box was too big, too square shouldered to wrap in the sweater vest. Strayhorn wanted to touch only newspaper as he extricated the frozen body, so when he finally got it placed in the center of the sweater and folded over the tattered gray edges, the package he made contained half newspaper which rustled like dry leaves when he pressed it against his chest.

Once he had it in his arms he couldn't put it down, so he struggled with his coat like a one-armed man, pulling and shrugging, till it shrouded him again. Not on really, but attached, so it dragged and flopped with a life of its own, animation that excited Daddy Garbage and gave him something to play with as he minced after Strayhorn and Strayhorn retraced his own footsteps, clutching the dead child to the warmth of his chest, moaning and blinking and tearing as the wind lashed his face.

An hour later Strayhorn was on Cassina Way hollering for John French. Lizabeth shooed him away with all the imperiousness of a little girl who had heard her mama say, "Send that fool away from here. Tell him your Daddy's out working." When the girl was gone and the door slammed behind her, Strayhorn thought of the little wooden birds who pop out of a clock, chirp their message and disappear. He knew Freeda French didn't like him. Not anything personal, not anything she could change or he could change, just the part of him which was part of what drew John French down to the corner with the other men to talk and gamble and drink wine. He understood why she would never do more than nod at him or say *Good day, Mr. Strayhorn* if he forced the issue by tipping his hat or taking up so much sidewalk when she passed him that she couldn't pretend he wasn't there. *Mr. Strayhorn*, and he been knowing her, Freeda Hollinger before she was Freeda French, for as long as she was big enough to walk the streets of Homewood. But he understood and hadn't ever minded till just this morning standing in the ankle-deep snow drifted up against the three back steps of John French's house next to the vacant lot on Cassina Way, till just this moment when for the first time in his life he thought this woman might have something to give him, to tell him. Since she was a mother she would know what to do with the dead baby. He could unburden himself and she could touch him with one of her slim, white-woman's hands, and even if she still called him *Mr. Strayhorn*, it would be alright. A little woman like that. Little hands like that doing what his hands couldn't do. His scavenging, hard hands that had been everywhere, touched everything. He wished Freeda French had come to the door. Wished he was not still standing tongue-tied and ignorant as the dog raising his hind leg and yellowing the snow under somebody's window across the way.

"Man supposed to pick me up first thing this morning. Want me to paper his whole downstairs. Seven, eight rooms and hallways and bathrooms. Big old house up on Thomas Boulevard cross from the park. Packed my tools and dragged my behind through all this snow and don't you know that white bastard ain't never showed. Strayhorn, I'm evil this morning."

Strayhorn had found John French in the Bucket of Blood drinking a glass of red wine. Eleven o'clock already and Strayhorn hadn't wanted to be away so long. Leaving the baby alone in that empty icebox of a shack was almost as bad as stuffing it in a garbage can. Didn't matter whose it was, or how dead it was, it was something besides a dead thing now that he had found it and rescued it and laid it wrapped in the sweater on the stack of mattresses where he slept. The baby sleeping there now. Waiting for the right thing to be done. It was owed something and Strayhorn knew he had to see to it that the debt was paid. Except he couldn't do it alone. Couldn't return through the snow and shove open that door, and do what had to be done by himself.

"Be making me some good money soon's I catch up with that peckerwood. And I'm gon spend me some of it today. Won't be no better day for spending it. Cold and nasty as it be outside, don't reckon I be straying too far from this stool till bedtime. McKinley, give this whatchamacallit a taste. And don't you be rolling your bubble eyes at me. Tolt you I got me a big money job soon's I catch that white man."

"Seems like you do more chasing than catching."

"Seems like you do more talking than pouring, nigger. Get your pop-eyed self on over here and fill us some glasses."

"Been looking for you all morning, man."

"Guess you found me. But you ain't found no money if that's what you looking for."

"Naw. It ain't that, man. It's something else."

"Somebody after you again? You been messing with somebody's woman? If you been stealin again or Oliver Edwards is after you again..."

"Naw, naw...nothing like that."

35

"Then it must be the Hell Hound hisself on your tail cause you look like death warmed over."

"French, I found a dead baby this morning."

"What you say?"

"Shhh. Don't be shouting. This ain't none McKinley's nor nobody else's business. Listen to what I'm telling you and don't make no fuss. Found a baby. All wrapped up in newspaper and froze stiff as a board. Somebody put it in a box and threw the box in the trash back of Dumferline."

"Ain't nobody could do that. Ain't nobody done nothing like that."

"It's the God awful truth. Me and Daddy Garbage on our way this morning up the alley. The dog, he found it. Turned over a can and the box fell out. I almost kicked it, John French. Almost kicked the pitiful thing."

"And it was dead when you found it?"

"Dead as this glass."

"What you do?"

"Didn't know what to do so I took it on back to my place."

"Froze dead."

"Laid in the garbage like wasn't nothing but spoilt meat."

"Goddamn . . ."

"Give me a hand, French."

"Goddamn. Goddamn, man. You seen it, sure nuff. I know you did. See it all over your face. God bless America . . . McKinley . . . Bring us a bottle. You got my tools to hold so just get a bottle on over here and don't say a mumbling word."

Lizabeth is singing to the snowman she has constructed on the vacant lot next door to her home. The wind is still and the big flakes are falling again straight down and she interrupts her slow song to catch snow on her tongue. Other kids had been out earlier, spoiling the perfect whiteness of the lot. They had left a mound of snow she used to start her snowman. The mound might have been a snowman before. A tall one, taller than any she could build because there had been yelling and squealing since early in the morning which meant a whole bunch of kids out on the vacant lot and meant they had probably worked together making a giant snowman till somebody got crazy or evil and smacked the snowman and then the others

36

would join in and snow flying everywhere and the snowman plowed down as they scuffled on top of him and threw lumps of him at each other. Till he was gone and then they'd start again. She could see bare furrows where they must have been rolling big snowballs for heads and bodies. Her mother had said: "Wait till some of those roughnecks go on about their business. Probably nothing but boys out there anyway." So she had rid up the table and scrubbed her Daddy's eggy plate and sat in his soft chair dreaming of the kind of clean, perfect snow she knew she wouldn't see by the time she was allowed out; dreaming of a ride on her Daddy's shoulders to Bruston Hill and he would carry her and the sled to a quiet place not too high up on the slope and she would wait till he was at the bottom again and clapping his hands and shouting up at her: "Go, go little gal."

"If you go to the police they find some reason put you in jail. Hospital got no room for the sick let alone the dead. Undertaker, he's gon want money from somebody before he touch it. The church. Them church peoples got troubles enough of they own to cry about. And they be asking as many questions as the police. It can't stay here and we can't take it back."

"That's what I know, John French. That's what I told you."

Between them the flame of the kerosene lamp shivers as if the cold has penetrated deep into its blue heart. Strayhorn's windowless shack is always dark except where light seeps through cracks between the boards, cracks which now moan or squeeze the wind into shrill whistles. The two men sit on wooden crates whose slats have been reinforced by stone blocks placed under them. Another crate, shortside down, supports the kerosene lamp. John French peers over Strayhorn's shoulder into the dark corner where Strayhorn has his bed of stacked mattresses.

"We got to bury it, man. We got to go out in this goddamn weather and bury it. Not in nobody's backyard neither. Got to go on up to the burying ground where the rest of the dead niggers is." As soon as he finished speaking John French realized he didn't know if the corpse was black or white. Being in Homewood, back of Dumferline wouldn't be anything but a black baby, he had assumed. Yet who in Homewood would have thrown it there? Not even those down home, country

37

Negroes behind Dumferline in that alley that didn't even have a name would do something like that. Nobody he knew. Nobody he had ever heard of. Except maybe crackers who could do anything to niggers, man, woman or child don't make no difference.

Daddy Garbage, snoring, farting ever so often, lay next to the dead fireplace. Beyond him in deep shadow was the child. John French thought about going to look at it. Thought about standing up and crossing the dirt floor and laying open the sweater Strayhorn said he wrapped it in. His sweater. His goddamn hunting sweater come to this. He thought about taking the lamp into the dark corner and undoing newspapers and placing the light over the body. But more wine than he could remember and half a bottle of gin hadn't made him ready for that. What did it matter? Black or white. Boy or girl. A mongrel made by niggers tipping in white folks' beds or white folks paying visits to black. Everybody knew it was happening every night. Homewood people every color in the rainbow and they talking about white people and black people like there's a brick wall tween them and nobody don't know how to get over.

"You looked at it, Strayhorn?"

"Just a little bitty thing. Wasn't no need to look hard to know it was dead."

"Can't figure how somebody could do it. Times is hard and all that, but how somebody gon be so cold?"

"Times is surely hard. I'm out there every day scuffling and I can tell you how hard they is."

"Don't care how hard they get. Some things people just ain't supposed to do. If that hound of yours take up and die all the sudden, I know you'd find a way to put him in the ground."

"You're right about that. Simple and ungrateful as he is, I won't be throwing him in nobody's trash."

"Well, you see what I mean then. Something is happening to people. I mean times was bad down home, too. Didn't get cold like this, but the cracker could just about break your neck with his foot always on it. I mean I remember my daddy come home with half a pail of guts one Christmas Eve after he work all day killing hogs for the white man. Half a pail of guts is all he had and six of us pickaninnies and my mama and grand-mama to feed. Crackers was mean as spit, but they didn't drive

38

people to do what they do here in this city. Down home you knew people. And you knew your enemies. Getting so you can't trust a soul you see out here in the streets. White, black, don't make no difference. Homewood changing...people changing."

"I ain't got nothing. Never will. But I lives good in the summertime and always finds a way to get through winter. Gets me a woman when I needs one."

"You crazy alright, but you ain't evil crazy like people getting. You got your cart and that dog and this place to sleep. And you ain't going to hurt nobody to get more. That's what I mean. People do anything to get more than they got."

"Niggers been fighting and fussing since they been on earth."

"Everybody gon fight. I done fought half the niggers in Homewood, myself. Fighting is different. Long as two men stand up and beat on each other ain't nobody else's business. Fighting ain't gon hurt nobody. Even if it kill a nigger every now and then."

"John French, you don't make no sense."

"If I make no sense out no sense, I be making sense."

"Here you go talking crazy. Gin talk."

"Ain't no gin talking. It's me talking and I'm talking true."

"What we gon do?"

"You got a shovel round here?"

"Got a broken-handled piece of one."

"Well get it, and let's go on and do what we have to do."

"It ain't dark enough yet."

"Dark as the Pit in here."

"Ain't dark outside yet. Got to wait till dark."

John French reaches down to the bottle beside his leg. The small movement is enough to warn him how difficult it will be to rise from the box. Nearly as cold inside as out and the chill is under his clothes, has packed his bones in ice and the stiffness always in the small of his back from bending then reaching high to hang wallpaper is a little hard ball he will have to stretch out inch by painful inch when he stands. His fist closes on the neck of the bottle. Raises it to his lips and drinks deeply and passes it to Strayhorn. Gin is hot in John French's mouth. He holds it there, numbing his lips and gums, inhaling the fumes. For a moment he feels as if his head is a balloon and someone is pumping it full of gas and there is a moment when the balloon is either going to bust or float off his shoulders.

"Gone, nigger. Didn't leave a good swallow." Strayhorn is talking with his mouth half covered by coatsleeve.

"Be two, three hours before it's good and dark. Sure ain't sitting here that long. Ain't you got no wood for that fire?"

"Saving it."

"Let's go then."

"I got to stay. Somebody got to be here."

"Somebody got to get another taste."

"Ain't leaving no more."

"Stay then. I be back. Goddamn. You sure did find it, didn't you?"

When John French wrestles open the door, the gray light enters like a hand and grasps everything within the shack, shaking it, choking it before the door slams and severs the gray hand at the wrist.

It is the hottest time of a July day. Daddy Garbage is curled beneath the big wheeled cart, snug, regal in the only spot of shade on the street at one o'clock in the afternoon. Every once in a while his ropy tail slaps at the pavement. Too old for most of his puppy tricks but still a puppy when he sleeps, Strayhorn thinks, watching the tail rise up and flop down as if it measures some irregular but persistent pulse running beneath the streets of Homewood.

"Mr. Strayhorn." The young woman speaking to him has John French's long, pale face. She is big and rawboned like him and has his straight, good hair. Or the straight, good hair John French used to have. Hers almost to her shoulders but his long gone, a narrow fringe above his ears like somebody had roughed in a line for a saw cut.

"Have you seen my daddy, Mr. Strayhorn?"

"Come by here yesterday, Miss French."

"Today, have you seen him today?"

"Hmmm . . ."

"Mr. Strayhorn, he has to come home. He's needed at home right away."

"Well now . . . let me see . . ."

"Is he gambling? Are they gambling up there beside the tracks? You know if they're up there."

"Seems like I might have seen him with a few of the fellows..."

"Dammit, Mr. Strayhorn. Lizabeth's having her baby. Do you understand? It's time, and we need him home."

"Don't fret, little gal. Bet he's up there. You go on home. Me and Daddy Garbage get him. You go on home."

"Nigger gal, nigger gal. Daddy's sure nuff fine sweet little nigger gal." Lizabeth hears the singing coming closer and closer. Yes, it's him. Who else but him? She is crying. Pain and happiness. They brought the baby in for her to see. A beautiful, beautiful little boy. Now Lizabeth is alone again. Weak and pained. She feels she's in the wrong place. She was so big and now she can barely find herself in the immense whiteness of the bed. Only the pain assures her she has not disappeared altogether. The perfect white pain.

She is sweating and wishing for a comb even though she knows she should not try to sit up and untangle the mess of her hair. Her long, straight hair. Like her mama's. Her Daddy's. The hair raveled on the pillow beside her face. She is sweating and crying and they've taken away her baby. She listens for footsteps, for sounds from the other beds in the ward. So many swollen bellies, so many white sheets and names she forgets and is too shy to ask again, and where have they taken her son? Why is no one around to tell her what she needs to know? She listens to the silence and listens and then there is his singing. *Nigger gal. Sweet, sweet little nigger gal.* Her Daddy's drunk singing floating toward her and a nurse's voice saying *no*, saying *you can't go in there* but her Daddy never missing a note and she can see the nurse in her perfect white and her Daddy never even looking at her just weaving past the uniform and strutting past the other beds and getting closer and singing, singing an ignorant, darky song that embarrasses her so and singing that nasty word which makes her want to hide under the sheets. But it's him and he'll be beside her and he'll reach down out of the song and touch her wet forehead and his hand will be cool and she'll smell the sweet wine on his breath and she is singing silently to herself what

41

she has always called him, always will, *Daddy John, Daddy John*, in time to the nigger song he chants loud enough for the world to hear.

"Got to say something. You the one likes to talk. You the one good with words." John French and Lemuel Strayhorn have been working for hours. Behind them, below them, the streets of Homewood are deserted, empty and still as if black people in the South hadn't yet heard of mills and mines and freedom, hadn't heard the rumors and the tall tales, hadn't wrapped packages and stuffed cardboard suitcases with everything they could move and boarded trains North. Empty and still as if every living thing had fled from the blizzard, the snow which will never stop, which will bury Dumferline, Tioga, Hamilton, Kelley, Cassina, Allequippa, all the Homewood streets disappearing silently, swiftly as the footprints of the two men climbing Bruston Hill. John French first, leaning on the busted shovel like it's a cane, stabbing the metal blade into the snow so it clangs against the pavement like a drum to pace their march. Strayhorn next, tottering unsteadily because he holds the bundle of rags and paper with both hands against his middle, thinking, when the wind gives him peace enough, of what he will say if someone stops him and asks him what he is carrying. Finally the dog, Daddy Garbage, trotting in a line straighter than usual, a line he doesn't waver from even though a cat, unseen, hisses once as the procession mounts higher toward the burying ground.

In spite of wind and snow and bitter cold, the men are flushed and hot inside their clothes. If you were more than a few feet away, you couldn't see them digging. Too much blowing snow, the night too black. But a block away you'd have heard them fighting the frozen earth, cursing and huffing and groaning as they take turns with the short-handled shovel. They had decided before they began that the hole had to be deep, six feet deep at least. If you had been close enough and watched them the whole time, you would have seen how it finally got deep enough so that one man disappeared with the tool while the other sat exhausted in the snow at the edge of the pit waiting his turn. You'd have seen the dark green bottle emptied and shoved neck first like a miniature headstone in the snow. You would have seen how one pecked at the stone hard ground

42

while the other weaved around the growing mound of snow and dirt, blowing on his fingers and stomping his feet, making tracks as random as those of Daddy Garbage in the untouched snow of the cemetery. . . .

"Don't have no stone to mark this place. And don't know your name, child. Don't know who brought you on this earth. But none that matters now. You your own self now. Buried my twins in this very place. This crying place. Can't think of nothing to say now except they was born and they died so fast too. But we loved them. No time to name one before she was gone. The other named Margaret, after her aunt, my little sister who died young too.

"Like the preacher say, May your soul rest in peace. Sleep in peace, child."

Strayhorn stands mute with the bundle in his arms. John French blinks the heavy snowflakes from his lashes. He hears Strayhorn grunt *amen* then Strayhorn sways like a figure seen underwater. The outline of his shape wiggles, dissolves, the hard lines of him swell and divide.

"How we gonna put it down there? Can't just pitch it down on that hard ground."

John French pulls the big, red plaid snot rag from his coat pocket. He had forgotten about it all this time. He wipes his eyes and blows his nose. Stares up into the sky. The snowflakes all seem to be slanting from one spot high over his head. If he could get his thumb up there or jam in the handkerchief, he could stop it. The sky would clear, they would be able to see the stars.

He kneels at the edge of the hole and pushes clean snow into the blackness. Pushes till the bottom of the pit is lined with soft, glowing fur.

"Best we can do. Drop her easy now. Lean over far as you can and drop her easy. . . ."

LIZABETH:
THE CATERPILLAR
STORY

DID you know I tried to save him once myself. When somebody was dumping ashes on the lot beside the house on Cassina Way. Remember how mad Daddy got. He sat downstairs in the dark with his shotgun and swore he was going to shoot whoever it was dumping ashes on his lot. I tried to save Daddy from that.

It's funny sitting here listening at you talk about your father that way because I never thought about nobody else needing to save him but me. Then I hear you talking and think about John French and know there ain't no way he could have lived long as he did unless a whole lotta people working real hard at saving that crazy man. He needed at least as many trying to save him as were trying to kill him.

Knew all my life about what you did, Mama. Knew you punched through a window with your bare hand to save him. You showed me the scar and showed me the window. In the house we used to live in over on Cassina Way. So I always knew you had saved him. Maybe that's why I thought I could save him too.

I remember telling you the story.

47

And showing me the scar.

Got the scar, that's for sure. And you got the story.

Thought I was saving Daddy, too, but if you hadn't put your fist through that window I wouldn't have had a Daddy to try and save.

Had you in my lap and we were sitting at the window in the house on Cassina Way. You must have been five or six at the time. Old enough to be telling stories to. Course when I had one of you children on my lap, there was some times I talked just to hear myself talking. Some things couldn't wait even though you all didn't understand word the first. But you was five or six and I was telling you about the time your Daddy ate a caterpillar.

The one I ate first.

The very one you nibbled a little corner off.

Then he ate the rest.

The whole hairy-legged, fuzzy, orange and yellow striped, nasty rest.

Because he thought I might die.

As if my babygirl dead wouldn't be enough. Huh uh. He swallowed all the rest of that nasty bug so if you died, he'd die too and then there I'd be with both you gone.

So he was into the saving business, too.

Had a funny way of showing it but I guess you could say he was. Guess he was, alright. Had to be when I look round and see all you children grown up and me getting old as sin.

Nineteen years older than me is all.

That's enough.

I remember you telling me the caterpillar story and then I remember that man trying to shoot Daddy and then I remember Albert Wilkes's pistol you pulled out from under the icebox.

That's a whole lot of remembering. You was a little thing, a lap baby when that mess in Cassina happened.

Five or six.

Yes, you were. That's what you was. Had to be because we'd been on Cassina two, three years. Like a kennel back there on Cassina Way in those days. Every one of them shacks full of niggers. And they let their children run the street half-naked and those burr heads ain't never seen a comb. Let them children out in the morning and called em in at night like they

48

was goats or something. You was five or six but I kept you on my lap plenty. Didn't want you growing up too fast. Never did want it. With all you children I tried to keep that growing up business going slow as I could. What you need to hurry for? Where you going? Wasn't in no hurry to get you out my lap and set you down in those streets.

I remember. I'm sure I remember. The man, a skinny man, came running down the alley after Daddy. He had a big pistol just like Albert Wilkes. And you smashed your fist through the glass to warn Daddy. If I shut my eyes I can hear glass falling and hear the shots.

Never knew John French could run so fast. Thought for a moment one of them bullets knocked him down but he outran em all. Had to or I'd be telling a different story.

It's mixed up with other things in my mind but I do remember. You told me the story and showed me the scar later but I was there and I remember too.

You was there, alright. The two of us sitting at the front window staring at nothing. Staring at the quiet cause it was never quiet in Cassina Way except early in the morning and then again that time of day people in they houses fixing to eat supper. Time of day when the men come home and the children come in off the streets and it's quiet for the first time since dawn. You can hear nothing for the first time and hear yourself think for the first time all day so there we was in that front window and I was half sleep and daydreaming and just about forgot I had you on my lap. Even though you were getting to be a big thing. A five- or six-year-old thing but I wasn't in no hurry to set you down so there we was. You was there alright but I wasn't paying you no mind. I was just studying them houses across the way and staring at my ownself in the glass and wondering where John French was and wondering how long it would stay quiet before your sister Geraldine woke up and started to fuss and wondering who that woman was with a baby in her lap staring back at me.

And you told the caterpillar story.

Yes, I probably did. If that's what you remember, I probably did. I liked to tell it when things was quiet. Ain't much of a story if there's lots of noise around. Ain't the kind you tell to no bunch of folks been drinking and telling lies all night. Sitting at the window with you at the quiet end of the afternoon was the right time for that story and I probably told it to wake myself up.

John French is cradling Lizabeth in one arm pressed against his chest. She is muttering or cooing or getting ready to throw up.

"What did she eat? What you saying she ate? You supposed to be watching this child, woman."

"Don't raise your voice at me. Bad enough without you frightening her."

"Give it here, woman."

His wife opens her fist and drops the fuzzy curled remnant of caterpillar in his hand. It lies there striped orange and yellow, dead or alive, and he stares like it is a sudden eruption of the skin of the palm of his hand, stares like he will stare at the sloppy pyramids of ash desecrating his garden-to-be. He spreads the fingers of the hand of the arm supporting the baby's back; still one minute, Lizabeth will pitch and buck the next. He measures the spiraled length of caterpillar in his free hand, sniffs it, strokes its fur with his middle finger, seems to be listening or speaking to it as he passes it close to his face. His jaws work the plug of tobacco; he spits and the juice sizzles against the pavement.

"You sure this the most of it? You sure she only ate a little piece?"

Freeda French is still shaking her head yes, not because she knows the answer but because anything else would be unthinkable. How could she let this man's daughter chew up more than a little piece of caterpillar. Freeda is crying inside. Tears glaze her eyes, shiny and thick as the sugar frosting on her Aunt Aida's cakes and there is too much to hold back, the weight of the tears will crack the glaze and big drops will steal down her cheeks. While she is still nodding yes, nodding gingerly so the tears won't leak, but knowing they are coming anyway, he spits again and pops the gaudy ringlet of bug into his mouth.

"I got the most of it then. And if I don't die, she ain't gonna die neither, so stop that sniffling." He chews two or three times and his eyes are expressionless vacant as he runs his tongue around his teeth getting it all out and down. . . .

Lizabeth: the Caterpillar Story

*   *   *

Someone had been dumping ashes on the vacant lot at the end of Cassina Way. The empty lot had been part of the neighborhood for as long as anybody could remember and no one had ever claimed it until John French moved his family into the rear end of the narrow row house adjoining the lot and then his claim went no farther than a patch beside the end wall of the row houses, a patch he intended to plant with tomatoes, peppers and beans but never got around to except to say he'd be damned if he couldn't make something grow there even though the ground was more rock and roots than it was soil because back home in Culpepper, Virginia, where the soil so good you could almost eat it in handfuls scooped raw from the earth, down there he learned about growing and he was going to make a garden on that lot when he got around to it and fix it to look nearly as good as the one he had loved to listen to when he was a boy sitting on his back porch with his feet up on a chair and nobody he had to bother with from his toes to the Blue Ridge Mountains floating on the horizon.

Ashes would appear in gray, sloppy heaps one or two mornings a week. The shape of the mounds told John French they had been spilled from a wheelbarrow, that somebody was sneaking a wheelbarrow down the dark, cobbled length of Cassina Way while other people slept, smothering his dream of a garden under loads of scraggly ash. One afternoon when Lizabeth came home crying with ash in her hair, hair her mother had just oiled and braided that morning, John French decided to put a stop to the ash dumping. He said so to his wife, Freeda, while Lizabeth wept, raising his voice as Lizabeth bawled louder. Finally goddamned somebody's soul and somebody's ancestors and threatened to lay somebody's sorry soul to rest, till Freeda hollering to be heard over Lizabeth's crying and John French's cussing told him such language wasn't fit for a child's ears, wasn't fit for no place or nobody but the Bucket of Blood and his beer drinking, wine drinking, nasty talking cronies always hanging round there.

So for weeks Lizabeth did not sleep. She lay in her bed on the edge of sleep in the tiny room with her snoring sister, afraid like a child is afraid to poke a foot in bath water of an uncertain temperature, but she was frozen in that hesitation not for an

51

instant but for weeks as she learned everything she could from the night sounds of Cassina Way, and then lay awake learning there was nothing else to learn, that having the nightmare happen would be the only way of learning, that after predictable grunts and alley clamors, the cobblestones went to sleep for the night and she still hadn't picked up a clue about what she needed to know, how she would recognize the sound of a wheelbarrow and find some unfrightened, traitorous breath in herself with which to cry out and warn the man who pushed the barrow of ashes that her father, John French, with his double-barrelled shotgun taller than she was, sat in ambush in the downstairs front room.

Even before she heard him promise to shoot whoever was dumping ashes she had listened for her Daddy to come home at night. He'd rummage a few minutes in the kitchen then she'd listen for the scrape of a match and count his heavy steps as he climbed to the landing; at *twelve* he would be just a few feet away and the candlelight would lurch on the wall and her father would step first to the girls' room, and though her eyes were squeezed as tightly shut as walnuts, she could feel him peering in as the heat of the candle leaned closer, feel him counting his daughters the way she counted the stairs, checking on his girls before he ventured the long stride across the deep well of the landing to the other side of the steps, the left turning to the room where her mother would be sleeping. Once in a while partying all by himself downstairs, he would sing. Rocking back and forth on a rickety kitchen chair his foot tapping a bass line on the linoleum floor, he'd sing, *Froggy went a courtin and he did ride, uh huh, uh huh*. Or the songs she knew came from the Bucket of Blood. His husky voice cracking at the tenor notes and half laughing, half swallowing the words in those songs not fit for any place but the Bucket of Blood.

Most times he was happy but even if she heard the icebox door slammed hard enough to pop the lock, heard his chair topple over and crash to the floor, heard the steps groan like he was trying to put his heel through the boards, like he was trying to crush the humpback of some steel-shelled roach with each stride, hearing even this she knew his feet would get quieter as she neared the end of her count, that no matter how long it took between steps when she could hear him snoring or shuffling back and forth along the length of a step like he

52

had forgotten *up* and decided to try *sideways*, finally he would reach the landing and the staggering light from the candle her mother always set out for him on its dish beside the front door would lean in once then die with the bump of her parents' door closing across the landing.

Lizabeth could breathe easier then, after she had counted him safely to his bed, after the rasp of door across the landing and the final bump which locked him safely away. But for weeks she'd lain awake long after the house was silent, waiting for the unknown sound of the wheelbarrow against the cobblestones, the sound she must learn, the sound she must save him from.

"It got to be that bowlegged Walter Johnson cause who else be cleaning people's fireplaces round here. But I'll give him the benefit of the doubt. Every man deserves the benefit of the doubt so I ain't going to accuse Walter Johnson to his face. What I'm gon do is fill the next nigger's butt with buckshot I catch coming down Cassina Way dumping ash."

She knew her father would shoot. She had heard about Albert Wilkes so she knew that shooting meant men dead and men running away and never coming back. She could not let it happen. She imagined the terrible sound of the gun a hundred times each night. If she slept at all, she did not remember or could not admit a lapse because then the hours awake would mean nothing. Her vigilance must be total. If she would save her father from himself, from the rumbling cart and the gray, ashy faced intruder who would die and carry her father away with him in the night, she must be constant, must listen and learn the darkness better than it knew itself.

"Daddy." She is sitting on his knee. Her eyes scale her father's chest, one by one she climbs the black buttons of his flannel shirt until she counts them all and reaches the grayish neck of his long johns. Their one cracked pearl button showing below his stubbled chin.

"Daddy. I want to stay in your hat."

"What you talking about, little sugar?"

"I want to live in your hat. Your big brown hat. I want to live in there always."

"Sure you can. Yes indeed. Make you a table and some chairs and catch a little squirrel too, let him live in there with you. Now that sounds like a fine idea, don't it? Stay under there till you get too big for your Daddy's hat. Till you get to be a fine big gal."

Lizabeth lowers her eyes from his long jaw, from the spot he plumped out with his tongue. He shifted the Five Brothers tobacco from one cheek to the other, getting it good and juicy and the last she saw of his face before her eyes fell to the brass pot beside his chair was how his jaws worked the tobacco, grinding the wad so it came out bloody and sizzling when he spit.

She was already big enough for chores and hours beside her mother in the kitchen where there was always something to be done. But hours too on the three steps her Daddy had built from the crooked door to the cobbled edge of Cassina Way. Best in the summer when she could sit and get stupid as a fly in the hot sun after it rose high enough to crest the row houses across the alley. If you got up before everybody else summer mornings were quiet in Cassina, nothing moving until the quiet was broken by the cry of the scissors-and-knife man, a jingling ring of keys at his waist, and strapped across his back the flintstone wheel which he would set down on its three legs and crank so the sparks flew up if you had a dull blade for him to sharpen, or by the iceman who would always come first, behind the tired clomp of his horse's hooves striking Cassina's stones. The iceman's wagon was covered with gray canvas that got darker like a bandage on a wound as the ice bled through. *Ice. Ice. Any ice today, lady?* The iceman sang the words darkly so Lizabeth never understood exactly what he cried till she asked her mother.

"He's saying *Any ice today, lady*, least that's what he thinks he's saying. Least that's what I think he thinks he's saying," her mother said as she listened stock-still by the sink to make sure. For years the iceman was Fred Willis and Fred Willis still owned the horse which slept some people said in the same room with him, but now a scowling somebody whose name Lizabeth didn't know, who wore a long rubber apron the color of soaked canvas was the one talking the old gray horse down the alley, moaning *Ice, ice, any ice today, lady* or whatever it was she heard first thing behind the hollow clomp of the hooves.

Stupid as a fly. She had heard her Daddy say that and it fit just how she felt, sun-dazed, forgetting even the itchy places on her neck, the cries of the vendors which after a while like everything blended with the silence.

Stupid as a fly during her nightlong vigils when she couldn't learn what she needed to know but she did begin to understand how she could separate into two pieces and one would listen for the wheelbarrow and the other part would watch her listening. One part had a Daddy and loved him more than anything but the other part could see him dead or dying or run away forever and see Lizabeth alone and heartbroken or see Lizabeth lying awake all night foolish enough to think she might save her Daddy. The watching part older and wiser and more evil than she knew Lizabeth could ever be. A worrisome part which strangely at times produced in her the most profound peace because she was that part and nothing else when she sat sun-drugged, stupid as a fly on the steps over Cassina Way.

Bracelets of gray soapsuds circled her mother's wrists as she lifted a china cup from the sink, rinsed it with a spurt of cold water and set it gleaming on the drainboard to dry. The same froth clinging to her mother's arms floated above the rim of the sink, screening the dishes that filled the bowl. Each time the slim hands disappeared into the water there was an ominous clatter and rattle, but her mother's fingers had eyes, sorted out the delicate pieces first, retrieved exactly what they wanted from the load of dishes. If Lizabeth plunged her own hands into the soapy water, everything would begin to totter and slide, broken glass and chipped plates would gnaw her clumsy fingers. Some larger pieces were handed to her to dry and put away which she did automatically, never taking her eyes from her mother's swift, efficient movements at the sink.

"Lizabeth, you go catch the iceman. Tell him five pounds."

Lizabeth shouted, *Five pound, we want five pound*. She knew better, her mother had told her a hundred times: pounds and miles, *s* when you talking bout more than one, but her Daddy said *two pound a salt pork* and *a thousand mile tween here and home* so when the wagon was abreast of the last row houses and the echo of the hooves and the echo of the blues line the iceman made of his call faded down the narrow funnel of Cassina Way she shouted loud as she could, *Five pound, five pound, Mister*.

The horse snorted. She thought it would be happy to stop

but it sounded mad. The driver's eyes went from the little girl on the steps to the empty place in the window where there should be a sign if anybody in the house wanted ice. When his eyes stared at her again, they said you better not be fooling with me, girl, and with a grunt much like the horse's snort he swung himself down off the wagon seat, jerked up an edge of the canvas from the ice and snapped away a five pound chunk in rusty pincers. The block of ice quivered as the iron hooks pierced its sides. Lizabeth could see splintered crystal planes, the cloudy heart of the ice when the man passed her on the steps. Under the high-bibbed rubber apron, the man's skin was black and glistening. He hollered once *Iceman* and pushed through the door.

If she had a horse, she would keep it in the vacant lot next door. It would never look nappy and sick like this one. The iceman's horse had bare patches in his coat, sore, raw-looking spots like the heads of kids who had ringworm. Their mothers would tie a stocking cap over the shaved heads of the boys so they could come to school and you weren't supposed to touch them because you could get it that way but Lizabeth didn't even like to be in the same room. Thinking about the shadowy nastiness veiled under the stockings was enough to make her start scratching even though her mother washed and oiled and braided her thick hair five times a week.

She waited till the wagon had creaked past the vacant lot before she went back inside. If her pinto pony were there in the lot, nibbling at the green grass her Daddy would plant, it would whinny at the sad ice wagon horse. She wondered how old the gray horse might be, why it always slunk by with its head bowed and its great backside swaying slowly as the dark heads of the saints in Homewood A.M.E. Zion when they hummed the verses of a hymn.

"That man dripping water in here like he don't have good sense. Some people just never had nothing and never will." Her mother was on her hands and knees mopping the faded linoleum with a rag.

"Here girl, take this till I get the pan." She extended her arm backward without turning her head. "Pan overflowed again and him slopping water, too." She was on her knees and the cotton housedress climbed up the backs of her bare thighs. Her mama's backside poked up in the air and its roundness, its splitness made her think of the horse's huge buttocks, then of her own narrow hips. Her mama drew the brimful drain pan from under the icebox, sliding it aside without spilling a drop. "Here," her arm extended again behind her, her fingers making the shape of the balled rag. She had to say *Here girl* again before Lizabeth raised her eyes from the black scarifications in the linoleum and pushed the rag she had wrung into her mother's fingers.

"I don't know why I'm down here punishing these bones of mine and you just standing there looking. Next time..."

Her mother stopped abruptly. She had been leaning on one elbow, the other arm stretched under the icebox to sop up the inevitable drips missed by the drain pan. Now she bowed her head even lower, one cheek almost touching the floor so she could see under the icebox. When her hand jerked from the darkness it was full of something blue-black and metal.

"Oh, God. Oh, my God."

She held it the way she held a trap that had snared a rat, and for a moment Lizabeth believed that must be what it was, some new rat-killing steel trap. Her mama set the wooden kind in dark corners all over the house but when one caught something her mother hated to touch it, she would try to sweep the trap and the squeezed rat body out the door together, leave it for John French to open the spring and shake the dead rodent into the garbage can so the trap could be used again. Her mama held a trap delicately if she had to touch it at all, in two fingers, as far from her body as she could reach, looking away from it till she dropped it in a place from which it could be broomed easily out the door. This time the object was heavier than a trap and her mama's eyes were not half-closed and her mouth was not twisted like somebody swallowing cod liver oil. She was staring, wide-eyed, frightened.

"Watch out... stand back."

On the drainboard the gun gleamed with a dull, blue-black light which came from inside, a dead glistening Lizabeth knew would be cold and quick to the touch, like the bloody, glass-eyed fish the gun lay next to.

"You've seen nothing. Do you understand, child? You've seen nothing and don't you ever breathe a word of this to a soul. Do you understand me?"

Lizabeth nodded. But she was remembering the man in the

alley. Must remember. But that afternoon in the kitchen it was like seeing it all for the first time. Like she had paid her dime to the man at the Bellmawr Show and sat huddled in the darkness, squirming, waiting for pictures to start flashing across the screen. It had to begin with the caterpillar story.

"I got the most of it then. And if I don't die, she ain't gonna die neither, so stop that sniffling."

Lizabeth has heard the story so many times she can tell it almost as well as her mother. Not with words yet, not out loud yet, but she can set the people—her father, her mother, herself as a baby—on the stage and see them moving and understand when they are saying the right words and she would know if somebody told it wrong. She is nearly six years old and sitting on her mother's lap as she hears the caterpillar story this time. Sitting so they both can look out the downstairs window into Cassina Way.

Both look at the gray covering everything, a late afternoon gray gathered through a fall day that has not once been graced by the sun. Palpable as soot the gray is in the seams between the cobblestones, seals the doors and windows of the row houses across the alley. Lights will yellow the windows soon but at this in-between hour nothing lives behind the gray boards of the shanties across the way. Lizabeth has learned the number *Seventy-Four-Fifteen* Cassina Way and knows to tell it to a policeman if she is lost. But if she is Lizabeth French, she cannot be lost because she will be here, in this house certain beyond a number, absolutely itself among the look-alikes crowding Cassina Way. She will not be lost because there is a lot next door where her Daddy will grow vegetables, and her mother will put them in jars and they will eat all winter the sunshine and growing stored in those jars and there are three wooden steps her Daddy made for sitting and doing nothing till she gets stupid as a fly in that same sun, and sleeping rooms upstairs, her sister snoring and the candle poked in before her Daddy closes the door across the deep well.

The end house coming just before the empty corner lot is Lizabeth and Lizabeth nothing more nor less than the thinnest cobweb stretched in a dusty corner where the sounds, smells and sights of the house come together.

Lizabeth watches her mother's eyes lose their green. She sits as still as she can. She is not the worm now like her mama

58

always calls her because she's so squirmy, she is nothing now because if she sits still enough her mother forgets her and Lizabeth who is nothing at all, who is not a worm and not getting too big to be sitting on people's laps all day, can watch the shadows deepen and her mama's green eyes turn gray like the houses across Cassina Way.

"There was a time Cassina Way nothing but dirt. Crab apple trees and pear trees grew where you see all them shacks. Then the war came and they had a parade on Homewood Avenue and you should have seen them boys strut. They been cross the ocean and they knew they looked good in their uniforms and they sure was gon let everybody know it. People lined up on both sides the street to see those colored troops marching home from the war. The 505 Engineers. Everybody proud of them and them strutting to beat the band. Mize well been dancing down Homewood Avenue. In a manner of speaking they were dancing and you couldn't keep your feet still when they go high stepping past. That big drum get up inside your chest and when Elmer Hollinger hits it your skin feels about to bust. All of Homewood out that day. People I ain't never seen before. All the ones they built these shacks for back here on Cassina Way. Ones ain't never been nowhere but the country and put they children out in the morning, don't call them in till feeding time. Let them run wild. Let them make dirt and talk nasty and hair ain't never seen a comb.

"That's why I'ma hold on to you, girl. That's why your mama got to be mean sometimes and keep you in sometime you want to be running round outdoors."

Lizabeth loves the quiet time of day when she can just sit, when she has her mama all to herself and her mama talks to her and at her and talks to herself but loud enough so Lizabeth can hear it all. Lizabeth needs her mother's voice to make things real. (Years later when she will have grandchildren of her own and her mother and father both long dead Lizabeth will still be trying to understand why sometimes it takes some-one's voice to make things real. She will be sitting in a room and the room full of her children and grandchildren and every-body eating and talking and laughing but she will be staring down a dark tunnel and that dark, empty tunnel is her life, a life in which nothing has happened, and she'll feel like scream-ing at the darkness and emptiness and wringing her hands

59

because nothing will seem real, and she will be alone in a roomful of strangers. She will need to tell someone how it had happened. But anybody who'd care would be long dead. Anybody who'd know what she was talking about would be long gone but she needs to tell someone so she will begin telling herself. Patting her foot on the floor to keep time. Then she will be speaking out loud. The others will listen and pay attention. She'll see down the tunnel and it won't be a tunnel at all, but a door opening on something clear and bright. Something simple which makes so much sense it will flash sudden and bright as the sky in a summer storm. Telling the story right will make it real.)

"Look at that man. You know where he been at. You know what he's been doing. Look at him with his big hat self. You know he been down on his knees at Rosemary's shooting crap with them trifling niggers. Don't you pay me no mind, child. He's your Daddy and a good man so don't pay me no mind if I say I wish I could sneak out there and get behind him and boot his butt all the way home. Should have been home an hour ago. Should have been here so he could keep an eye on you while I start fixing dinner. Look at him just sauntering down Cassina Way like he owns it and got all the time in the world. Your sister be up in a minute and yelling soon as her eyes open and him just taking his own sweet time.

"He won too. Got a little change in his pocket. Tell by the way he walks. Walking like he got a load in his pants, like other people's nickels and dimes weigh him down. If he lost he'd be smiling and busting in here talking fast and playing with youall and keep me up half the night with his foolishness. Never saw a man get happy when he gambles away his family's dinner. Never saw a man get sour-faced and down in the mouth when he wins."

Lizabeth doesn't need to look anymore. Her Daddy will get closer and closer and then he'll come through the door. Their life together will begin again. He is coming home from Rosemary's, down Cassina Way. He is there if you look and there if you don't look. He is like the reflection, the image of mother and daughter floating in the grayness of Cassina Way. There if she looks, there if she doesn't.

She stares at the pane of glass and realizes how far away she has been, how long she has been daydreaming but he is only a few steps closer, taking his own good time, the weight of somebody else's money in his pockets, the crown of his hat taller than the shadowed roofs of Cassina Way.

Her mama's arms are a second skin, a warm snuggling fur that keeps out the grayness, the slight, late-afternoon chill of an October day. She hums to herself, a song about the caterpillar story her mama has just told. Her baby sister is sleeping so Lizabeth has her mother to herself. Whenever they are alone, together, is the best time of the day, even if it comes now when the day is nearly over, sitting at the window in her mama's lap and her mama, after one telling of the caterpillar story, quiet and gray as Cassina Way. Because Lizabeth has a baby sister Geraldine she must love even though the baby makes the house smaller and shrinks the taken-for-granted time Lizabeth was used to spending with her mama. Lizabeth not quite six that early evening, late afternoon she is recalling, that she has not remembered or relived for five years till it flashes back like a movie on a screen that afternoon her mother pulls the revolver from under the icebox.

Her mother screams and smashes her fist through the windowpane. A gunshot pops in the alley. Her Daddy dashes past the jagged space where the windowpane had been, glass falling around his head as he bounds past faster than she has ever seen him move, past the empty, collapsing frame toward the vacant lot. A gun clatters against the cobbles and a man runs off down the corridor of Cassina Way.

My God. Oh, my God.

Her mama's fist looks like someone has tied bright red strings across her knuckles. The chair tumbles backward as her mother snatches her away from the jagged hole. Baby Geraldine is yelping upstairs like a wounded animal. Lizabeth had been daydreaming, and the window had been there between her daydream and her Daddy, there had been separation, a safe space between, but the glass was shattered now and the outside air in her face and her mama's hand bleeding and her mama's arms squeezing her too tightly, crushing her as if her small body could stop the trembling of the big one wrapped around it.

"Lizabeth . . . Lizabeth."

When her mama had screamed her warning, the man's eyes leaped from her Daddy's back to the window. Lizabeth saw

61

the gun but didn't believe the gun until her mama screamed again and flung her fist through the glass. That made it real and made her hear her own screams and made her Daddy a man about to be shot dead in the alley.

If a fist hadn't smashed through the window perhaps she would not have remembered the screaming, the broken glass, the shots when she watched her mama drag a pistol from under the icebox and set it on the bloody drainboard.

But Lizabeth did remember and see and she knew that Albert Wilkes had shot a policeman and run away and knew Albert Wilkes had come to the house in the dead of night and given her father his pistol to hide, and knew that Albert Wilkes would never come back, that if he did return to Homewood he would be a dead man.

"You're a fool, John French, and no better than the rest of those wine-drinking rowdies down at the Bucket of Blood and God knows you must not have a brain in your head to have a gun in a house with children and who in the name of sense would do such a thing whether it's loaded or not and take it out of here, man, I don't care where you take it, but take it out of here." Her mother shouting as loud as she ever shouts like the time he teased her with the bloody rat hanging off the end of the trap, her Daddy waving it at her mama and her mama talking tough first, then shouting and in tears and finally her Daddy knew he had gone too far and carried it out the house. . . .

Lizabeth remembered when the gun was dragged from under the icebox so there was nothing to do but lie awake all night and save her Daddy from himself, save him from the trespassing cart and smoking ashes and the blast of a shotgun and dead men and men running away forever. She'd save him like her mama had saved him. At least till he got that garden planted and things started growing and he put up a little fence and then .nobody fool enough to dump ashes on something belonged to John French.

You ought to paint some yellow stripes and orange stripes on that scar, Mama.

Don't be making fun of my scar. This scar saved your father's life.

I know it did. I'm just jealous, that's all. Because I'll never know if I saved him. I'd sure like to know. Anyway an orange and yellow caterpillar running across the back of your hand would be pretty, Mama. Like a tattoo. I'd wear it like a badge, if I knew.

Don't know what you're talking about now. You're just talking now. But I do know if you hadn't been sitting in my lap, I'da put my whole body through that window and bled to death on those cobblestones in Cassina Way so just by being there you saved me and that's enough saving for one day and enough talk too, cause I can see John French coming down that alley from Rosemary's now and I'm getting sad now and I'm too old to be sitting here crying when ain't nothing wrong with me.

HAZEL

■▪■▪■▪■▪■▪■▪■▪■▪■▪■▪■▪■▪■▪■

"Don't worry bout what hates you. What
loves you's what you got to worry bout…"
Bess

THE day it happened Hazel dreamed of steps. The black steps her brother Faun had pushed her down. The white steps clinging to the side of the house she would not leave till she died. Down the steep black stairwell you always fell faster and faster. In the first few moments of the dream you could count the steps as parts of your body cracked on each sharp, wooden edge. But soon you were falling so fast your body trailed behind you, a broken, rattling noise like tin cans tied to a wedding car. The white steps were up. You mounted them patiently at first. The sun made them gleam and printed their shadow black against the blank, clapboard wall. If you looked up you could see a pattern repeated endlessly to the sky. A narrow, slanted ladder of nine steps, a landing, another bank of bare, bone white railings and steps leaning toward the next landing. Patiently at first, step by step, but then each landing only leads you to another flight of steps and you have been climbing forever and the ground is too far away to see but you are not getting any closer to the top of the building. The sun dazzles you when you stop to catch your breath. You are dizzy, exposed. You must hurry on to the next landing. You realize you cannot stop.

You understand suddenly that you are falling *up* and this dream is worse than your brother's hands flinging you down into the black pit.

"Eat your peas now, honey." Her mother was busy halving peas into neat green hemispheres so Hazel wiggled her tongue at the ones prepared for her, the ones her mother had shoved with the edge of her knife into a mound in one compartment of her plate. They're good and juicy her mother said as she speared another pea. Can hardly catch them, she said as she sliced the pea and its two halves disappeared in the gray soup covering the bottom of the plate's largest section. Her mother boiled everything and always splashed water from pan to plate when she portioned Hazel's meals into the thick, trisected platter. If my food had those little wings like fish it could swim to me, Hazel thought. I'd put my lips on my plate and open my mouth wide like the whale swallowing Jonah and my food just swim to me like that.

"Here's the rest now. You eat up now." The knife squeaked through the flood, driving split peas before it, tumbling them over the divider so the section nearest Hazel was as green as she remembered spring.

"Have a nice breast of lamb cooking. By the time you finish these, it'll be ready, darling."

So green she wanted to cry. Hazel wished she knew why her tears came so easily, so suddenly over nothing. She hated peas. Her mother boiled them till the skins were loose and wrinkled. Pure mush when you bit into them. And who ever heard of cutting peas in half. *So you don't choke, darling. Mama doesn't want to lose her baby. Can't be too careful.* She had screwed up her face and stuck out her tongue at the peas just a moment before when her mother wasn't looking but now she felt like crying. Mushy and wrinkled and wet didn't matter at all. She didn't want to disturb the carpet of green. Didn't want to stick her fork in it. It was too beautiful, too green. A corner of spring in the drab room she would never leave.

Her mother never gets any older. She's slim, dainty, perfect as she rises and crosses to the stove, a young girl from the back, her trim hips betraying no sign of the three children they've borne. The long, straight hair they say she inherited from her mother Maggie is twisted and pinned into a bun on top of her head. A picture of Maggie they say when she lets

it down and gathers it in her hands and pulls it forward and
lets it fall over one shoulder the way Maggie always wore hers.
Grandmother Maggie in the oval photograph on the mantelpiece. That's your grandmother, Hazel. Looks like a white
lady, don't she? She could sit on her hair. Black and straight
as any white woman's. Liked to let it hang like it is in the
picture. She'd sit and play with it. Curl the end round her
fingers. *That's your grandmother. It's a shame she didn't live
long enough for you to see her. But she was too delicate, too
beautiful. God didn't make her for living long in this world.*

Not one gray hair in the black mass when her mother swept
it over her shoulder, two handfuls thick when her mother Gaybrella pulled and smoothed the dark river of hair down across
her breast. Like a river or the wide, proud tail of a horse.

If her mother was not getting older, then she must be getting
younger, Hazel thought, because nobody stood still. Hazel
knew no one could stand still, not even a person who lives in
a chair, a person who is helpless as a little baby, a person who
never leaves the house. Even if you become Hazel, a person
like that, you can't stand still. Some days took a week to pass.
Some nights she'd awaken from her dreams and the darkness
would stun her, would strike her across her mouth like a blow
from a man's fist and she'd sink down into a stupor, not awake
and not asleep for dull years at a time. She knew it hurt to have
children, that women sweated and shrieked to wring life out
of their bodies. That's why they called that hard, killing work
labor, called it a woman's bed of pain. She knew it hurt to
have a child dragged from your loins but it couldn't be any
worse than those nights which were years and years ripped
away from the numb cave of nothingness which began at her
waist.

You couldn't stand still. You got older and more like a
stone each day you sat in that chair, the chair which had been
waiting at the foot of the stairs your brother pushed you down.
So her mother was growing younger, was a girl again in her
grace, in her slim body crossing to the stove and raising the
lid to check the boiling breast of lamb.

"It's getting good and tender. It's almost done." Lamb smell
filled the room, the shriveled pea halves were already cold to
the touch. Hazel mashed one under her finger. As she wiped
the mush on the napkin beside her plate she wondered what

God used to clean his hands. How He got her off his thumb after he had squashed her in the darkness at the bottom of the steps.

The day it happened she dreamed of steps and thought of swallowing peas and chewing the lamb her mother Gaybrella had boiled to tastelessness. Until the day it roared beside her Hazel had never seen death. Death to her was that special look in her mother's eyes, a sneaky, frightened look which was not really something in the eyes but something missing, the eyes themselves missing from her mother's face. Death was her mother's eyes hiding, hiding for a whole morning, a whole afternoon, avoiding any encounter with Hazel's. Someone had knocked at the door early and Hazel had heard voices in her sleep. Her mother had shushed whoever it was and by the time Hazel was awake enough to listen the whispering on the other side of the door had stopped. Then the outside door was shut and bolted, a woman's footsteps had clattered down the three flights of outside steps and a strange something had emptied her mother's eyes. Hazel hadn't asked who had arrived at dawn, or asked what news the visitor had carried. She hadn't asked because there was no one to ask. Sometimes their three rooms at the top floor of Mr. Gray's house seemed smaller than a dress mother and daughter were struggling to wear at the same time. But the day of the empty eyes her mother found a million places in the tiny rooms to hide. Hazel had hummed all the songs she knew to keep herself company. By two o'clock her nervousness, the constant alert she forced herself to maintain had drained her. She was ready to cry or scream and did both when her mother had appeared from the bedroom in her long black coat. Her mother never left the house alone. Once or twice a year on Ferd's arm she might venture down into the Homewood streets but never alone. With her head tied in a scarf and her body wrapped from ankles to chin in the column of black she had faced Hazel for the first time that day. Her mother Gaybrella had looked like a child bundled up for an outing on a winter day. A child whose wide eyes were full of good-bye.

She's leaving me. She's going away. The words were too terrible to say. They were unthinkable but Hazel couldn't think anything else as she had stared at the pale girl woman who had once been her mother, who was too young now to be her mother, at the child who was going away forever.

"It's John French, sugar." Her mother's eyes had gone again. There was no one to ask why, or how long, no one but her own pitiful, crippled self in the room she would never leave. John French was a big, loud, gentle man who brought her candy and fruit. Her mother smiled at him in a way Hazel had never seen her smile before. Those kisses he planted on Hazel's forehead each time he left smelled of wine and tobacco. Coming and going he'd rattle the three flights of stairs which climbed the outside of Mr. Gray's clapboard house.

"You don't come on down outa here like you got good sense, Gay, I'ma come up and get you one day. Drag you if I have to. Fine woman like you cooped up here don't even see the light of day. I'ma come up here and grab you sure enough."

John French who was an uncle or an in-law or whatever you were to somebody when he married your mother's niece. Cousin Freeda who was Gert's girl. Aunt Gert and Aunt Aida and Aunt Bess your mother's sisters. John French had daughters who would be relatives too. Nice girls he said. *I'ma get those hussies come to see you some time.* How many years had it been since he said that. How many years before Lizabeth knocked on Sunday morning. She said it was Sunday and said she was just stopping by on her way home from church. And said her Daddy said hello. And said he's not doing so well. Heart and all and won't listen to the doctor. My Daddy's hard-headed, stubborn as a mule, she said. How many years ago and Lizabeth still coming, still dropping by on Sundays to say hello. That's how you know it's a Sunday. Lizabeth knocking in her Sunday clothes and, Hi, how you all doing? That's how you know Sunday still comes and comes in winter when she wears a big coat and in summer when she's sweating under her Sunday clothes. She'll take off the little hats she wears and set them on the table. In spring they look like Easter baskets. Girl, it's hot out there. Phew, she'll say and stretch out her legs. Ain't fit for a dog out there. Aunt Gay, she'll say. You should have heard Miss Lewis this morning. She can still sing, Aunt Gay. Old as she is she can still get that whole church shouting. You ought to come the next time she's singing. She always does a solo with the Gospel Chorus and they're on

every third Sunday. You ought to come and I'll stay here with
Hazel. Or Hazel could come too. We could get somebody to
help her down the steps. We could get a wheelchair and somebody would give us a ride. Why don't both you'all come next
third Sunday?

John French in Lizabeth's face. His high cheekbones and
long jaw. White like her Daddy and his French eyes and the
good French hair he used to have and she still does. Lizabeth
is like John French always worrying them to come down into
the world. A girl then a woman. The years pretty on her.
Lizabeth can get up when she's finished with her tea in winter
or her lemonade in summer, get up and walk away on two
strong legs so the years do not pile up on her. She does not
lose them by the fistful in the middle of the night and wake
up years older in the morning. Lizabeth is not a thousand years
old, she is not a stone heavy with too many years to count.

It's John French, sugar. Her mother had never said more
than that. Just stood there in her long black coat, in the body
of that child she was becoming again. Stood there a moment
to see if her silence, her lost eyes might do what she knew
words couldn't. But silence and eyes staring through her,
around her, hadn't checked Hazel's sobs so Gaybrella left and
tiptoed down the three flights of steps and returned in two
hours, tiptoeing again, easing the door open and shut again,
saying nothing as she shed the black coat and washed her hands
and started water boiling for dinner.

Death was that something missing in her mother Gaybrella's
eyes. Death was her mother leaving to go to John French,
leaving without a word, without any explanation but Hazel
knowing exactly where she was going, and why and knowing
if her mother ever leaves that way again it will be death again.
It will be Aunt Aida or Aunt Bess if she leaves again, if there
is anyone else who can make her tip down the steps, make her
lose her eyes the way John French did.

The day it happened (the *it* still unthinkable, unsayable as
it was when her mother stood draped in black on the threshold)
began with Bess *yoo-hooing* from the yard behind Mr. Gray's
house.

"Yoo-hoo. Yoo-hoo, Gay." Little Aunt Bess yodeling up
from the yard. That made it Tuesday because that's when Aunt
Bess came to do the wash. First the dream of steps, of black

72

steps and white steps, then the day beginning with Aunt Bess hollering "*Yoo-hoo*. What you got today? it's Tuesday. What you got for me?"

Her mother hated to drop the bundle of laundry into the yard but short-legged Bess hated all those steps and since she was the one doing the favor she'd yoo-hoo till she got her sister's attention and got her on the landing and got the bundle sailing down to her feet.

"Oww. Look at that dust. Look at that dust lapping at my things. If they weren't dirty before, they're dirty now."

"You wouldn't be dropping them down here if they wasn't dirty in the first place. I know you're the cleaningest woman in the world sister Gaybrella, but you still get things dirty."

"Let's not have a conversation about my laundry out here in public."

"Ain't no public to it. Ain't nobody here but us chickens. This all you got for me, Gay?"

"I can do the rest."

"Just throw it all down here. Don't make no sense for you to be doing no rest."

"You know I can't do that. You know I don't let anybody touch the rest."

"You can be downright insultin sometimes. Holding on to them few little things like you don't trust your own sister or something. And me bending over your wash every week."

"If it's too much trouble, I'll do it all myself. Just bring it back up here and I'll do it all myself."

"Shut up, woman. I've been doing it all these years. What makes you think I'ma stop today?"

"Then you know I can't give you everything. You know I have to do our private things myself."

"Suit yourself. Mize well run my head against a brick wall as try to change your ways. If you got sheets in here I'll have to hang them on this line. Won't have room on mine today."

"Go ahead. You know I dry the little business I have right up here."

"Say hello to that sweet angel, Hazel. *Yoo-hoo*, Hazel. You hear me girl?"

"She hears you, Bess. The whole neighborhood hears you."

"What I care about some neighborhood, I'm saying hello to my angel and anybody don't like it can kiss my behind."

"Please Bess."

"Don't be pleasing me. Just throw the rest of your dirty clothes down here so I can go on my way. Don't you be washing today. Don't do it today."

"I'm going inside now. Thank you."

"And don't you be thanking me. Just listen to me for once and don't be washing youall's underwear and hanging it over that stove."

"Good-bye."

And the door slams over Bess's head. She yells again. *Don't wash today*, but not loud enough to carry up the three flights of steps. She is bending over and pulling the drawstrings of the laundry bundle tighter so there is enough cord to sling the sack over her back. She is a short, sturdy-legged, reddish-yellow woman. Her skin is pocked with freckles. No one would guess she is the sister of the ivory woman who dropped the bundle from the landing. Bess hefts the sack over her shoulder and cuts catty-corner through the backyards toward the intersection of Albion and Tioga and her washing machine.

It happened on a Tuesday because her mother slammed the door and came in muttering about that Bess, that uncouth Bess. Her tongue's going to be the death of that woman. She married below her color but that's where her mouth always wanted to be anyway. Out in the street with those roughnecks and field-hands and their country nigger ways. Her mother Gaybrella just fussing and scolding and not knowing what to do with her hands till she opened the wicker basket in the bathroom where she stored their soiled private things and ran the sink full of water and started to wash them out. That calmed her. In a few moments Hazel could hear her humming to herself. Hear the gentle lapping of the water and the silk plunged in again and again. Smell the perfumed soap and hear the rasp of her mother's knuckles as she scrubbed their underthings against the washboard.

A warm breeze had entered the room while her mother stood outside on the landing talking to Bess. A spring, summer breeze green as peas. It spread like the sunlight into every corner of the room. Hazel could see it touching the curtains, feel it stirring the hair at the nape of her neck. In the chair she never left except when her mother lifted her into bed each night Hazel tried to remember the wind. If she shut her eyes and held her palms over her ears she could hear it. Pulled close to the window she could watch it bend trees, or scatter leaves or see snowflakes whirl sideways and up in the wind's grasp. But hearing it or watching it play were not enough. She wanted to remember how the wind felt when you ran into it, or it ran into you and pasted your clothes to your skin, and tangled your hair into a mad streaming wake and took your breath away. Once she held her cupped hands very close to her face and blew into them, blew with all her might till her jaws ached and tears came. But it wasn't wind. Couldn't bring back the sensation she wanted to remember.

"Mama." Her mother is stringing a line above the stove. Their underthings have been cleaned and wrung into tight cylinders which are stacked in the basin her mother set on the sideboard.

"Bess never did listen to Mama. She was always the wild one. A hard head. She did her share of digging Mama an early grave. Mama never could do anything with her. Had a mind of her own while she was still in the cradle. I don't know how many times I've explained to her. There are certain things you wear close to your body you just can't let anybody touch. She knows that. And knows better than to be putting people's business in the street."

"Mama."

"What's that honey?"

"Could you set me on the landing for a while?"

"Honey I don't trust those stairs. I never did trust them. As long as we've been here I've been begging Mister Gray to shore them up. They sway and creak so bad. Think you're walking on a ship sometimes. I just don't trust them. The last time I went down with Ferdinand I just knew they wouldn't hold us both. I made him go first and held on to his coattail so we both wouldn't have to be on the same step at the same time. Still was scared to death the whole way down. Creaking and groaning like they do. Wouldn't trust my baby out there a minute."

"Is it warm?"

"In the sun, baby."

"I won't fall."

"Don't be worrying your mama now. You see I got these things to hang. And this place to clean. And I want to clean myself up and wash my hair this morning. Don't want to be looking like an old witch when Bess comes back this afternoon with the laundry. We can't slip, darling. We have to keep ourselves neat and clean no matter what. Doesn't matter what people see or don't see. What they never see are the places we have to be most careful of. But you know that. You're my good girl and you know that."

"If the sun's still out when you finish, maybe . . ."

"Don't worry me. I have enough to do without you picking at me. You just keep me company awhile. Or nap if you're tired."

Hazel watched as piece by piece her mother unrolled and pinned their underclothes on the line stretched above the stove. The back burners were lit. Steam rose off the lace-frilled step-ins and combinations.

"I have a feeling Ferdinand will come by today. He said last time he was here he was being fitted for a new suit and if I know my son it won't be long before he has to come up here to his mama and show off what he's bought. He's a good son. Never lost a night's sleep worrying over Ferdinand. If all mothers' sons were sweet as that boy, bearing children wouldn't be the burden it surely is. It's a trial. I can tell you it's a trial. When I look at you sitting in that chair and think of the terrible guilt on your other brother's shoulders, I can't tell you what a trial it is. Then I think sometimes, there's my little girl and she's going to miss a lot but then again she's blessed too because there's a whole lot she'll never have to suffer. The filth and dirt of this world. The lies of men, their nasty hands. What they put in you and what they turn you into. Having their way, having their babies. And worst of all expecting you to like it. Expecting you to say *thank you* and bow down like they're kings of the world. So I cry for you, precious. But you're blessed too. And it makes my heart feel good to know you'll always be neat and clean and pure."

It was always "your other brother" when her mother spoke of Faun. She had named him and then just as carefully unnamed him after he pushed his sister down the stairs. Her mother was the one who blamed him, who couldn't forgive, who hadn't said his name in fifteen years. There was Ferdinand and "your other brother." Hazel had always shortened her brother's names. To her they had been Ferd and Faun from the time she could speak. Her mother said every syllable distinctly and cut her eyes at people who didn't say *Fauntleroy* and *Ferdinand*. I gave my sons names. Real names. All niggers have nicknames. They get them everywhere and anywhere. White folks. Children. Hoodlums and ignorant darkies. All of them will baptize you in a minute. But I chose real names for my boys. Good, strong names. Names from their mother and that's who they'll be in my mouth as long as I live. But she was wrong. Fauntleroy became "your other brother." Faun had forced his mother to break her promise to herself.

Ferd was a timid, little man, a man almost dandified in his dress and mannerisms. He was nearly as picky as their mother. He couldn't stand dust on his shoes. His watch chain and the gold eagle head of his cane always shone as if freshly polished. A neat, slit-eyed man who pursed his lips to smile. When he sat with them he never looked his sister in the eye. He'd cross his leg and gossip with his mother and drink his tea from the special porcelain cups, never set out for anyone but him. Hazel knew he didn't like their mother. Never adored her the way she and Faun always did. To him Gaybrella was never a fairy princess. As a child he made fun of her strange ways. Once he had pursed his lips and asked them: If she's so good, if she's so perfect, why did Daddy leave her? But daddies had nothing to do with fairy princesses and they giggled at the silliness of his question. Then, like their father, Faun had run away or been run away, and ever since in Ferd's voice as he sat sipping tea and bringing news of the world, Hazel could hear the sneer, the taunt, the same mocking question he had asked about their father, asked about the absent brother. Hazel knew her mother also heard the question and that her mother saw the dislike in Ferd's distant eyes but instead of ordering him from the room, instead of punishing him the way she punished Faun for the least offense, she doted on Ferdinand. His was the only arm she'd accept, the only arm she'd allow to lead her down into the streets of Homewood.

Faun was like the wind. There were days when Hazel said his name over and over to herself. Never Fauntleroy but *Faun*. Faun. She'd close her eyes and try to picture him. The sound of his name was warm; it could lull her to sleep, to daydreaming of the times they ran together and talked together and shared a thousand secrets. He was her brother and the only man she had ever loved. Even as a girl she had understood that any other man who came into her life would be measured against Faun. Six days a week he killed animals. He always changed his clothes at work but Hazel believed she could smell the slaughterhouse blood, could feel the killing strength in his hands when he pinched her cheek and teased her about getting prettier every day. Her big brother who was like the wind. Changeable as the wind. But his mood didn't matter; just staying close to him mattered. That's why they fought. Why they raged at each other and stood inseparable against the world. So when he was twenty and full of himself and full of his power over other women and she was seventeen and learning what parts of him she must let go and learning her own woman powers as he rejected them in her and sought them in others, when they rubbed and chafed daily, growing too close and too far apart at once, the fight in the kitchen was no different than a hundred others, except his slaughterhouse hands on her shoulders pushed harder than he meant to, and her stumbling, lurching recoil from a blow she really didn't feel much at all, was carried too far and she lost her balance and tumbled through the kitchen door someone had left unlocked and pitched down the dark steep stairwell to Mr. Gray's second floor where the chair was waiting from which she would never rise.

"I expect him up those stairs anytime." Her mother had let her hair down. It dangled to her waist, flouncing like the broad, proud tail of a horse as she swept the kitchen floor.

Then it happened. So fast Hazel could not say what came first or second or third. Just that it happened. The unspeakable, the unsayable acted out before her eyes.

A smell of something burning. Almost like lamb. Flames crackling above the stove. Curling ash dropping down. Her mother shouting something. Words or a name. A panicked look back over her shoulders at the chair. Hazel forever in the chair. Then flames like wings shooting up her mother's back. Her mother wheeling, twisting slim and graceful as a girl. Her mother Gaybrella grabbing the river of her hair and whipping it forward over her shoulders, and the river on fire, blazing in her fists. Did her mother scream then or had she been screaming all along? Was it really hair in her hands or the burning housecoat she was trying to tear from her back? And as she rushed past Hazel like a roaring, hot wind, what was she saying, who was she begging for help? When her mother burst through the door and crashed through the railing into thin air who was she going to meet, who was making her leave without a word, without an explanation.

Fifteen years after the day it happened, fourteen years after Hazel too, had died, Lizabeth rode in the ambulance which was rushing with sirens blaring to Allegheny County Hospital. She was there because Faun was Gaybrella's son and Hazel's brother and she had stopped by all those Sundays and was one of the few who remembered the whole story. She had heard Faun had returned to Homewood but hadn't seen him till one of the church sisters who also possessed a long memory asked her if she knew her cousin was sick. So Lizabeth had visited him in the old people's home. And held his hand. And watched the torment of his slow dying, watched his silent agony because the disease had struck him dumb. She didn't know if he recognized her but she visited him as often as she could. A nurse called the ambulance when his eyes rolled to the top of his head and his mouth began to foam. Lizabeth rode with Faun in the screaming ambulance so she was there when he bolted upright and spoke for the first time in the two months she had been visiting him. "I'm sorry...I'm so sorry," was what he said. She heard that plainly and then he began to fail for the last time, tottering, exhausting the last bit of his strength to resist the hands of the attendants who were trying to push him back down on the stretcher. She thought he said, *Forgive me*, she thought those were Faun's last words but they sputtered through the bubbling froth of his lips and were uttered with the last of his fading strength so she couldn't be sure.

THE CHINAMAN

▪▲▪▲▪▲▪▲▪▲▪▲▪▲▪▲▪▲▪▲▪▲▪▲▪▲▪▲▪▲▪

The toasts—long, bawdy, rhymed narratives invented by black street bards—contain much new slang but also preserve older words and ways of speaking. In the toasts the Chinaman appears as a symbol of decay and death.

See *Toasts*—
Wm. Labov *et al*.

OUTSIDE her window the last snow of the season is white only until it touches the pavement. Freeda's thoughts are her thoughts only until they reach the cloudy pane of glass where they expire silently, damp as tears, like snow against asphalt.

To believe who she is Freeda must go backward, must retreat, her voice slowly unwinding, slowly dismantling itself, her voice going backward with her, alone with her as the inevitable silence envelops. Talking to herself. Telling stories. Telling herself.

Once ... once ... her first baby born premature and breathless. The snow falling and her cousin May snatches away the child from the others who have shrieked, keened, moaned and are already beginning to mouth prayers for the dead. The door slams, shaking the wooden row house on Cassina Way, shattering the calm the women's folded hands and bowed heads are seeking. They realize the still, blue baby is gone. And that May is out there in the snow like a crazy woman with the dead child in her arms and ain't took time for coat or nothing she'll catch her death too in the blizzard that has its hand inside the house now and flings the door again and again crashing against its frame.

Once ... how many years ago ... Freeda was a baby then, she was forgiving then, burying her head in the wet pillow, hiding her eyes from theirs because she does not want to read the death of her firstborn in the women's faces. She wants to forgive. Forgive John French for the nights he loved her. Forgive the eyes of the women who smiled knowingly when she complained, who showed her their scars and wrinkled flesh, who said *Jesus* and smiled, and winced when she did and said *Everything's gon be all right, child* and *Thank Jesus* and *Ain't she beautiful she carries high like her mama, Gert* and *Her skin's so pretty,* and *Eat, honeychild, eat everything you want you eating for two now*. Who held her hand and rubbed her back and trudged through the snow to boil water and boil rags and stand on tired feet when it was time for her baby to come.

But their eyes are not the eyes of children. She cannot believe they knew everything else and didn't know the baby was twisted wrong side down in her belly. Freeda passes her gaze from one face to the other. They were ready to pray. They had been praying all along so they knew all along and she couldn't forgive. If someone would press her face down into the pillow she would turn blue like her baby was blue. The women's sorrowing, helpless faces would go away. She could forgive them. Her aunts, her neighbors, her cousin May, a girl like she is still a girl. Freeda knows their faces better than she knows her own. She hates what hovers sorrowing in their eyes.

Freeda hears the women rush away. The ragged, noisy lift of a flock of pigeons scared from the sidewalk. They are abandoning her. They were mountains rimming the valley of her pain. They were statues, stiff as the mourning women huddling over the broken body of Jesus in the picture in the Sunday school corner of Homewood A.M.E. Zion Church. Now they are fleeing and she is alone. Not even her baby beside her, if there was a baby borne to her by that sea of pain.

May... May... They are shouting through the open door.

May is kneeling in the snow across Cassina Way where it has drifted waist deep. She hunches forward shielding the baby from the wind, while she plunges its naked body into the snow. She must turn her face into the wind to see the others. Her hair,

her eyebrows and cheeks are caked with white. She is a snow
witch and nobody moves a step closer. She hollers something
at them which the wind voids.

Then May struggles to her feet, and stomps back through
the gaping door with the baby in her arms. She is praising Jesus
and Hallelujahing and prancing the floor before anybody can
grab the door and get it shut behind her.

"Wouldn't be for that I be telling a different story altogether.
Yes indeed. She so tiny could fit in a shoebox. Naw, I ain't
lying. If I'm lying, I'm flying. It's the God's truth, sure enough.
Didn't weigh but a pound and a half. Weeniest little thing you
ever did see. Called her mite. You know like little mighty mite.
Course there was something else in that name too. Couldn't
help but think that little girl child *might* make it and she *might*
not. And everybody scared to call her anything but *mite*. Such
a tiny little thing. Feed her with one of them eye droppers.
Didn't sleep or nap less it be on somebody's bosom so she stay
warm. Little thing curl up just like an eensy-beensy monkey,
curl up right on your chest with that thumb in her mouth. The
cutest thing. She got that little thumb and gone. Couldn't hardly
see the nails on her fingers they so tiny."

The firstborn, Lizabeth, our mother, saved by May in the
snow. May's told the story a hundred times but each time it's
new and necessary. If she didn't tell the story right, there would
be no baby shuddering to life in her arms when she runs through
the crashing door. There would be no Lizabeth, none of us
would be gathered in my grandmother's house on Finance Street
listening to May tell how Geraldine came next. And then the
boy, Carl, birthed by my grandmother. Making it all seem so
easy. Spring born. Bright and cleansing like the new rain sluic-
ing along the curb. A boybaby in Freeda's arms, plump and
crying. Peace. As if his coming was a promise to her of how
it would always be. How it should be easy. So when the twins
came and died, one at birth, the other named Margaret after
Daddy John's sister, holding on a week, whatever peace
brought by the first son was shattered, broken and strewn in
Freeda's path like bits of glass, like the dry, splintered bones
in the Valley of the Shadow she must cross in her bare feet as
her body swells again and again life and death share her belly.
Finally Martha. Four then. The seasons passing. The children
real then. As real as his weight on her body. John French

pressing her down into the starched sheets, her body a leaf between the pages of a book. Sometimes, straightening the bed, when she pulls back the homemade quilt she sees her form etched in the whiteness. She touches her edges, her hollows, smooths the wrinkles, pats the indentations, laying her hands where his have been, finding herself as she leans over the sprawled figure his bulk has pressed into the sheets.

Because she knows one day she will roll back the patchwork, velvet-edged, storytelling quilt and there will be nothing. Because her body's outline not deepened by his weight is only a pale shadow, a presence no more substantial than what might be left by a chill wind passing over the sheet.

Freeda watches the snow beat noiselessly against the window. Watches it disappear like the traces of her body when she pounds the white sheet. The faces of the women gather around her again, but they are older now, wrinkle old, gray old, like her own face last time she saw it in the oval mirror of the oak dresser at the foot of their bed. She calls it *their* bed even though she knows the faces, crowded and stomped down as the sooty hills on which Homewood is dying, have come to tell her John French is gone. If you are just a child and marry a man, one day you will grow up and the man will be gone. He can't wait and you can't hurry. Even though trying hard to hurry and to wait are the best part of your love, what makes your love better than what passes for love around you. One day he'll be gone and that will be that. Twice your age when he stole you. Twice your age when he sat with his elbows on his knees and his shoulders hunkered and his eyes downcast, sprawled all arms and legs on the stool in your Aunt Aida's front room while you said to her in the back room where she and Uncle Bill slept, I'm married now and she said, Yes you are now. I can tell just looking at you. John French married you good. Married you real good, didn't he? Saying the words so they hurt so you felt brazen like the ungrateful wench and hussy she didn't say you were. Not calling any names. Not fussing but saying the words so *married* was a door slammed, so *married* was the ashes of all those years Aunt Aida and Uncle Bill had sacrificed to raise her. John French is quiet as she's ever seen him in her life till Aunt Aida leaves her in the dark little bedroom and whispers something to her man Bill and Uncle Bill goes to the closet and gets not the shotgun he had loaded and set inside there but his jug of whiskey and two glasses and pours and hands one to John French.

Yes, she wants to scream. Of course he's dead. What else is he supposed to be with me lying up here an old woman. He was too big to move wedged between the seat of the toilet and the edge of the bathtub. She had heard him fall all the way from the kitchen and flew up the steps two and three at a time getting to him. Ain't no room to put my knees, he'd grumble. Shame when a man can't even squat right in his own house. She crashed open the door with both hands. She had heard him groan once while she rushed up the steps but he lay still now and her heart leaping in her chest was the only sound in the bathroom. But when she clambered on her knees under the sink so she could touch him and raise his face from the pool of vomit spreading on the linoleum she could hear the pipes gurgle and the leaky guts of the toilet hissing. She did as much as she could before she ran to the door and screamed into Cassina Way for help.

It was Fred Clark who came first. Who helped her drag John French from between the toilet and the tub that was always bumping his knees. He must have died while she was at the door because he was dead weight when they lifted him and dead when they laid him across *their* bed.

Someone always comes...Homewood people are good about coming. And they're best about coming around when there's nothing they can do. When someone's dead and the faces hovering around you are like flowers cut for a funeral. Fred Clark came and then Vernetta sent that useless pigeon-toed man of hers and they got John French laid across *their* bed. And Vernetta Jones down at the bottom of the steps moaning, *Have mercy, Have mercy.* Moaning it like you know she's gon moan it everytime she tells the story she can't wait to tell about John French dying in the bathroom and *I heard Freeda screaming for help and sent Ronald over there and I was so shocked you know how much I done prayed for John French to do right I was so shocked I couldn't even get up the steps I just stood at the bottom praying God have mercy, God have mercy cause I knowed he was dead.*

Freeda counts the faces. There are three. But then there are

87

three more and three more and more threes than she can count above her. Then there is one face hiding behind the others. A face the others cannot see because they stare down at her, stare with their eyes full of tears and their mouths full of prayers so they never see the yellow face grinning behind them, the man who is the only man in the room, the Chinaman with his shriveled yellow walnut of a face. He laughs at her, he is the only one who knows she knows John French is long dead.

The curled edge of the clawfoot tub and the bottom of the sink are cold as she crawls to him. Her feet sneak away and run naked into the snow. Once she had dreamed it would happen this way. A cold, white dream which made her shiver long after she awakened. In the dream the Chinaman sat on a fence. He flashed teeth like gold daggers and laughed and laughed at his ownself trying to make a dollar out of fifteen cents. Chinky, chinky, Chinaman and she was laughing too but then he started to melt, started to run down out of the funny pajama-looking suit he was wearing. Then his face blew up like a watermelon. The skin got fatter and fatter so it swoll up and closed his eyes and closed his mouth and all the rest of him just yellow water running down the fence. And she knew she shouldn't be laughing. Knew that he wasn't laughing at himself but at what was going to happen to her when he finished melting and all the insides of him exploded through that big moon face. She began to shiver when she realized the face was filled with something cold. Like snow only it would be the color of the stuff leaking down out of his pant legs, that pee color and oily like that stuff only cold, colder than anything she had ever touched, cold so the icy pieces of jelly when they flew against her body would turn her to stone.

Three months had passed since my grandmother's death. I had flown to Pittsburgh alone to her funeral. When I returned home I hadn't said much about her. The weather in Pittsburgh had been cold and damp. On the day of the funeral it rained. There wasn't much to say about all of that, about the gray streets and somber gray hills crowded with ramshackle houses and the gray people shrouded in raingear or huddling under umbrellas. I couldn't talk about that because it was too depressing, and I couldn't talk about the storytelling and whiskey all night after we buried my grandmother either. You had to be part of the whole thing to understand why we could laugh and get high while Aunt May, tucked back into an overstuffed chair so her stockinged feet barely touched the rug, told us the stories of Homewood. Our laughter wouldn't seem appropriate unless you had been there through everything and heard how she was saying what she was saying. So I didn't talk much when I got home. I let the trip slowly seep inside me. Sipped it without really tasting it the way I sipped Jim Beam that night May told stories.

Our family had begun its annual migration East. Five hundred miles the first day and another three hundred next day before a flat. There had been a sickening swerve and I hit the brake too hard and lost control but luckily just for an instant and then the Custom Cruiser let me guide it onto the shoulder of the highway. As I began the process of changing the tire, which meant first unpacking a summer's worth of luggage to get at the spare in the back of the station wagon and finding one piece of the jack missing, and cursing the American way of leaving little things out, the sky over my shoulder had divided itself neatly into a layer of dense gray and one of luminous, spooky whiteness. The dark half above squeezing light out of the sky; all the energy in the band of white squirming and heating up as it is compressed into a smaller and smaller space. Then drum rolls of thunder and jagged seams of light splitting the darkness.

We were in Iowa. One of those featureless stretches of Interstate 80 which are a way of getting nowhere fast. Judy yelled at me to get inside the car. She has a morbid fear of lightning so I feel it's my duty to cure her, to treat thunderstorms with disdain and nonchalance and survive. So I take my good time stuffing in the last few boxes and suitcases I had unloaded. The highway would buckle each time a semi passed. I winced every time, stepping backward, swaying in the blast of hot air as the trucks exploded just a few feet away. That sudden caving in of the earth scared me more than the threat of thunderbolts delivered from the sky.

The first rain drops were as big as eggs. Not falling but flung in handfuls so they struck inside the station wagon spattering the bags before I could get the tailgate shut. Behind the

89

wheel again I dried my hands, face and the back of my neck. I felt like I had been running a long time, running fast and strong and the exhilaration of my body had made me slightly breathless, a little giddy.

"Why are you so foolish? Why did you stay out there till the last minute?"

"You wouldn't believe me if I told you."

"It's not funny. Look at the boys. You've managed to terrify them acting like a fool." In the faces of the children strapped in their carseats behind us I could see the echo of their mother's fear, an immense silence welling behind their eyes.

But it was good in a way. The steady drumming on the roof, the windows steamed shut, the windblown sheets of rain suddenly splashing against the metal skin. All hell breaking loose outside, but we were inside, cocooned, safe, together. I liked the isolation, the sudden detour. "Hey, you guys. It's like being in a space ship. Let's pretend we're on our way to Mars. Prepare for blast-off."

And there was the business of assigning roles, the squabbles over rank, the exact determination of a noise level for our rocket motors which would not encourage the migraine Judy felt coming on.

But we were launched successfully from that Iowa plain. Though we were knee deep in water, some of our controls smoking and sputtering, our ark rose, shuddering in the girdle of rain but quickly through it, gathering speed and thrusting pure and swift wherever....

So I could relinquish the controls and shut off the intercom and plead the weariness of six days exploring a virgin planet, battling the Dictosaurs, the Todals, the men whose heads grow beneath their shoulders. The ship was safe in other hands so I could shut my eyes and listen to the rockets purr calmly through the Intergalactic night.

That's when I saw her. When my grandmother, Freeda, came to me. She is wearing a thin, gray cardigan, buttonless, perhaps another color once, mauve perhaps as I look more closely or perhaps the purplish blue of the housedress beneath the worn threads gives the wool its suggestion of color. The sleeves of the sweater are pushed back from her wrists. One long hand rests in her lap. The skin on the back of her hand seems dry and loose. If she tried to lift anything heavier than the hand to which it was attached, her fragile wrist protruding from the cuffed and frayed sweater sleeve would snap. She sits in her wooden rocker in front of the fireplace which has been covered over with simulated-brick Contact paper. Just over her head is the mantelpiece crowded with all of our pictures. The television set is muttering a few feet away. Bursts of laughter and applause. Dull flickers of light as the image twitches and rolls. She reaches inside the front of her dress and fumbles with a safety pin which secures the handkerchief cached there against her underclothes. Lilies hidden beneath her dress. Lilies spreading in her lap as she unties the knotted corners of the flowered handkerchief. In the center of the handkerchief a few coins and two or three bills folded into neat squares, one of which she opens as slowly as she had opened the silk. When she learned to talk again after her second stroke, she could only manage a minimal movement of her lips. Her head moves from side to side with the effort of producing the strange, nasal, tonal language of rhythms and grunts. If you listened closely, you could detect the risings and fallings of familiar sentence patterns. The words blurred and elided but you could get the message if you listened.

Take it. Take it. Take it, Spanky. I am leaving home. The first one in the family to go off to college. She thrusts the money in my hand. *Take it. Go on, boy.* A five-dollar bill as wrinkled and criss-crossed as the skin at the corners of her eyes.

Over the wind and rain and rockets and the cars driven by madmen still careening past on the invisible highway I hear her offering the money . . . the strange, haunted whine I would write if I could.

Three months after her death and finally it was time. I needed to talk about her. The storm deserted us. We limped to a gas station and they fixed the flat and promised they'd have a whole jack for us next morning. We decided to stop for the night just down the road a ways in the place the mechanic had recommended, a Holiday Inn overlooking the Mississippi River. After the kids were asleep I began to talk about my grandmother. I wished for May's voice and the voices of my people in a circle amening and laughing and filling in what I didn't know or couldn't remember, but it was just me whispering in the dark motel room, afraid to wake my sons.

91

For sixteen years they took care of her. My Aunt Geraldine and Uncle Carl, the only son. The other girls, my mother and her sister Martha, had married. Within a week after her husband's death Freeda had a stroke, almost dying, and though her body recovered, her will did not. Wanting only to follow her dead husband everybody said. To be with John French they all said. Yet she was still their mother. And they still lived under her roof, so for sixteen years Geraldine and Carl nursed the shell she had become. The last year of her life she spent mainly in the hospital. She had stopped moving and seldom talked. Her blood thickened so there was always the threat of pneumonia or a clot that needed watching. Endless shots and medicines which might achieve three or four lucid hours a week. During her last month at home before the final confinement in Allegheny Hospital she became deeply agitated. Like a light bulb which glows unnaturally bright just before it pops, she seemed to improve. Her eyes were animated again, she struggled to speak and be listened to. My Aunt Geraldine and Uncle Carl were excited. Talked of miraculous remissions, reprieves, God changing his mind in the eleventh hour. Even though it was terror filling her eyes, even though her gestures and nasal keening described a phantom who had begun to prey on her.

Carl understood the word first, the sound Freeda had begun to repeat constantly. For weeks it had remained a mystery, part of her improved condition, part of her terror. Then, with the certainty of something known all along, Carl matched a word to the sound. A word not discovered but remembered. He couldn't believe the word had escaped him so long once he matched it to the sound she had been shaping. *Chinaman*. When he repeated it back to her the first time aloud, her chin dropped to her chest. A gagging sound came from her throat. As if the word summoned a Chinaman, diabolical and menacing beside the rocker. *Chinaman. Chinky, chinky Chinaman, sitting on a fence. Trying to make a dollar out of fifteen cents*. Hiding in corners. Hovering over her bed at night. Pulling her clothes awry. Raking his nails across her face and hands, inflicting the red wounds she showed them in the morning.

Of course he followed her to the hospital. Every member of the family knew him. The Chinaman's vigil as faithful as the shifts of relatives who tended my grandmother as she lay dying. She slept most of the time. Drugged. Too fatigued to lift her eyelids. I began disbelieving in her. I was glad I was far away and didn't have to trek to the hospital. But the others were faithful. They did the bathing, the touching, the holding on till nothing else remained. It was to them she complained of the Chinaman. But against the background of her slow, painful dying, the Chinaman became for the family a figure of fun. Mama's Chinaman. They talked about him like a dog. Transformed him into an aged suitor courting her with flowers, candy and teenage awkwardness. Made fun of him. Told stories about his appearances and disappearances, his clothes, his hiding places, how he whistled at the nurses and pinched their behinds. The Chinaman became a sort of Kilroy for the family. His signature turning up in unexpected places. His name implicated in any odd or obscene occurrence in the hospital.

One day they moved an Oriental man into a room down from my grandmother's ward. The people in my family became acquainted with his people, sharing cigarettes and gossip in the visitors' lounge. Since both patients slept most of the day, the social gatherings in the lounge offered an opportunity to exchange commiserations, but also a chance to return to the world of health and well-being without totally deserting the realm of the sick. . . .

But the story was stiff, incomplete. I said I'd tell the rest when Judy felt better. She fell asleep quickly but I heard paddle-wheeled steamers packed with cotton and slaves ply the river all night long.

Two more days on the road. Then we are in my mother's kitchen. The house is quiet. Relatives and friends in and out all day as always during our summer visits. It's good to see everybody but the days are long and hot and busy so it's also good when the last person leaves. My mother, Lizabeth, and my wife and I are in the kitchen. It's after twelve and the house is quiet. *Five things*, my mother says. *Five things in my life I'll never forget*. One was Faun asking forgiveness in the ambulance. She doesn't tell us what the other three are, but she does tell us about the Chinaman.

"Carl and I were sitting with Mama at the hospital. It must have been around six because I heard them collecting the dinner trays. She had had a bad day. I still don't know how she lasted as long as she did. Her arms weren't any bigger around than this . . . there just wasn't anything left . . . how she held on I'll never know. She had been coughing all day and they were always worried about it getting in her lungs. Anyway we were kinda down and just sitting listening to the awful rattling in her sleep when he walked in leaning on the arm of his daughter. She was a nice girl. We always talked in the lounge. She was steady about coming to see her father. You could tell she was really worried about him and really cared. A pretty girl, too. Well, she only brought him as far as the door. I guess she heard Mama sleeping and how quiet we were so she just waved from there and sort of whispered her father was going home in the morning and good luck. And the old Chinaman peeked around into the room. I guess he was curious about Mama so he poked his head in and looked at her and then they were gone. That's all. Stopped to say good-bye just like we would have said good-bye to them if we could have taken Mama home out of that place.

"Mama never woke up again. She died early the next morn-ing and when I walked down the hall with the nurse I looked in that Chinese man's room and it was empty.

"That's just the way it happened. I was there, I know. He peeked in and Mama never woke up again. I can't tell you how many times I've asked myself how she knew. Because Mama did know. She knew that Chinaman was coming for her. That he'd tip in her door one day and take her away. Things like that happen in people's lives. I know they do. Things you just can't explain. Things that stay with you. Not to the day I die will I understand how Mama knew, but I do know things like that don't just happen. Five times in my life I've been a witness and I don't understand but I'm sure there's a plan, some kind of plan."

I am sleepy but the story gets to me the way it did the first time I heard it. My mother has told it, finished it like I never can. And the shape of the story is the shape of my mother's voice. In the quiet house her voice sounds more and more like May's. My mother doesn't wave her arms like May or rise and preacher-strut like May when May gets the spirit. My mother's hands drum the table edge, or slowly the fingertips of one hand stroke and pull and knead those of the other. For her the story of the Chinaman is a glimpse of her God who has a plan and who moves in mysterious ways. For me the mystery of the Chinaman is silence, the silence of death and the past and lives other than mine.

I watch my mother's pale fingers shuttle in and out of one another. I watch my wife slip into her own quietness, distant and private. The silence is an amen.

THE WATERMELON STORY

THE first time he saw somebody get their arm chopped off was in front of the A&P on Homewood Avenue. They used to pile watermelons outside at the alley corner of the store. A big plate glass window where they stuck Sale signs and Specials This Week signs and propped church posters and advertisements for this and that on the bottom inside ledge was at that end of the store too. A window starting almost on the sidewalk and running up twice as tall as a man so they needed long ladders to wash it when they used to try and keep things clean in Homewood. Watermelons would be there piled three and four high, the green ones shiny, the striped ones cool as if the sunshine couldn't ever melt those pale veins of ice shooting through their rinds. Mostly the winos would stay over in the trees, below the tracks in the Bums' Forest during the heat of the day but sometimes you'd get one straying off, too high or too dry to care, and then he'd wander up where people doing their shopping, wander through there stumbling or singing or trying to get his hands on somebody's change till he got tired of people looking through him and at him and church ladies snorting and kids laughing like the circus was in town or staring like he was some kind of creature from Planet X and then he'd just settle hisself in a piece of shade where the settling looked good and nobody'd mind him no more than they would a cat or dog sleeping under the porch. But the one he saw with his arm hanging by bloody threads, dangling so loose the man in the white apron had to hold the weight of it so it wouldn't just roll on down between the watermelons, that wino had decided for some reason to sit on the stack of melons in front of the A&P.

Must have nudged one of the front ones, the bottom ones holding the stack together and when they all started to rolling like big fat marbles under him he must have leaned back to catch hisself and they pitched him through that plate glass window. Like trying to walk on marbles. Must have been like that. His legs going out from under him all the sudden and him full of Dago Red and dozing in that July sun so he was probably dreaming something and the dream got snoring good to him and Homewood Avenue a thousand miles away. Like having the rug jerked out from under your feet and you know you're falling, know you're going to hit the ground so you throw your arm back to catch yourself and ain't the ground you catch but a whole A&P windowful of glass slicing down on your shoulder.

Must have been easy at first. I mean your fist punches through real quick and busts a clean hole and your arm just passes right on through too. Ain't bleeding, ain't even scratched, it's through that tunnel real easy and quick and nothing hurts, you don't even know you're in trouble, specially with all that sweet wine and sun and you're just waiting for the goddamn watermelons to stop acting a fool so your feet and your behind can find the pavement but then that glass comes down like a freight train, snaps shut like a gator's jaws and you know, you know without looking, without feeling the pain yet either, you know it got you and that screaming behind your ear is not falling, crashing glass anymore, it's you waking up and saying hello and saying good-bye to your arm.

Must have been like that even though he didn't see it happen and he wasn't the man. He dreamed it like that many years later and the dream was his, the throne of watermelons belonged to him, green and striped and holding the heat of the sun. And when it topples and topples him with it into the bath of cool glass, the shattering glass is there ringing like a cymbal in his ear even after he opens his eyes. He dreamed it that way and often without warning when he was walking down the street his shoulder muscle would twitch, would tremble and jerk away from the ax in its dream. Like his arm was living on borrowed time and knew it. The shock of seeing a severed arm in the white aproned lap of the man who had run from inside the store meant that arms didn't have to stay where they were born. Nothing had to stay the way it was. He had wondered if all that blood soaking the apron was wino blood or if the bald white man kneeling beside the hurt wino had brought pig blood and cow blood and blood from lambs and wall-eyed fish from inside the store. Was the man surrounded by the green sea of melons a butcher, a butcher who was used to bloody parts and blood spattered clothes, a butcher cradling the wino's arm so the last few threads won't break. Is he whispering to the wino, trying to help him stay still and calm or is the wino dreaming again, moaning a song to the lost arm in his dream.

The A&P is gone now. They scrubbed the blood from the pavement and stopped stacking watermelons on the sidewalk. One of the grown-ups told him later the wino's life had been saved by a tourniquet. Somebody in the crowd had enough sense to say Forget about that thing. Forget about trying to stick that arm back on and had ripped the apron into strips and made a tourniquet and tied it around the stump to stop the bleeding. That saved him. And he had wanted to ask, Did anybody save the arm, but that sounded like a silly question, even a smart-alecky question, even when he said it to himself so instead he imagined how the only black man who worked in the A&P, Mr. Norris who always sat two rows down toward the front of Homewood A.M.E. Zion Church, pushed his iron bucket that was on wheels through the wide double doors of the A&P. The melons had skittered and rolled everywhere. People trying to get closer to the blood had kicked holes in some, some had plopped over the curb and lay split in the gutter of Homewood Avenue. A few of the biggest melons had walked away when folks crowded around. But it wasn't Mr. Norris's job to count them and it wasn't, he told the produce

manager, his job to scrabble around Homewood Avenue picking watermelons, wasn't no part of his job, Mr. Norris told
him again as he hummed Farther Along and slopped soapy
water on the dark splotches of blood. Mr. Norris had made a
neat, rectangular fence of watermelons in front of the broken
window to keep fools away. Nobody but a fool would get close
to those long teeth of glass, jag-edged teeth hanging by a thread,
teeth subject to come chomping down if you breathe on them
too hard. Mr. Norris had kept his distance and gingerly swept
most of the glass into a corner of his watermelon yard. Then
the bucket and mop. When the pavement dried he'd sprinkle
some sawdust like they have behind the fish counter. There
were smears of blood and smears of watermelon and he'd dust
them all. He slooshed the heavy mop up and back, up and
back, digging at the worst places with soapy water.

Rather than ask a question nobody would answer and nobody
would like, he imagined Mr. Norris taking his own good time
cleaning the mess off the sidewalk. Though ninety-nine percent
of the shoppers were black, Mr. Norris was the only black man
working for the A&P, and that made him special, made him
somebody people watched. Mr. Norris had rules. Everybody
knew what they were and understood his slowness, his peculiar
ways were part of his rules. Watching his hands or his face or
the poses he struck, you'd think he was leading an orchestra.
The way he carried himself had nothing to do with wiping
shelves or scrubbing floors or carting out garbage unless you
understood the rules and if you understood the rules, and understood they came from him, then everything he did made sense
and watching him you'd learn more than you would from asking
dumb questions and getting no answers.

They wouldn't have left the arm for Mr. Norris to broom
up. They'd know better so of course they'd take it with them,
wherever they took the wino, wherever they took the tourniquet, the stump, the bloody strips of apron.

Don't try to stick it back on. Leave that damn thing be and
stop the bleeding.

He hadn't been there when the one man with good sense
had shouted out those words. He didn't see how you wrapped
a stump, how you put on a handle so you could turn off the
blood like you turn off a faucet. Turn and quit. He thought

that's what she said at first. Those words made sense at first till she explained a little bit more and told him not "turn and quit," it's *tourniquet*, like you learn in first aid or learn in the army or learn wherever they teach one another such things. Then she said, Uggh. I couldn't do it. I couldn't get down there with my hands in all that mess. They'd have to carry me away if I got too close to it. Me, I wouldn't be no more good. But thank God somebody with good sense was there, somebody with a strong stomach to do what have to be did.

As he listened he heard May saying the words and remembered it was her then. May who told the story of the accident and then told him later, No, he didn't die. He lost that arm but he's still living, he's still back up in the Bum's Forest drinking just as much wine with one arm as he did with two.

And May's story of the lost arm reminded her of another story about watermelons. About once there was a very old man Isaac married to an old woman Rebecca. Was in slavery days. Way, way back. Don't nobody care nothing about those times. Don't nobody remember them but old fools like me cause I was there when Grandpa told it and I ain't never been able to forget much, least much of what I wanted to forget. Well I was there and he told me how it was way back then. There was this Isaac and Rebecca and they was old when it started. Old before those olden days way back, way, way back. It was Africa you see. Or Georgy or someplace back there it don't make no difference no way. Niggers be niggers anyplace they be. If you get my meaning. But this old man and old woman they be living together ninety-nine years and they's tired and they ain't got child the first to hold they old heads, they's childless you see. Old lady dry as a dry well and always was and looks like she's fixin to stay the very same till Judgment Day. So they was some old, sad people. Had some good times together, everybody got good times once in a while, and they was good to each other, better to each other than most people be these days. He'd still pat them nappy knots up under her head rag. She'd rub that shoulder of his been sore for fifty years when he come in from the fields at night. They was good to each other. Better than most. They did what they could. But you ain't never too young nor too old be hurt. And a hurt lived with them all the days of their lives, lived every day from can to caint in that itty bitty cabin in the woods. They loved God and wasn't scared of dying. Naw, they wasn't feared of that like some sinners I know. And they wasn't ungrateful niggers neither. And I could name you some them, but I ain't preaching this morning. I'm telling youall a story bout two old people didn't never have no babies and that's what hurt them, that's what put that sadness on they hearts.

Youall heard bout Faith? Said I wasn't preaching this morning but youall heard that word, ain't you? Ain't asking if you understand the word. I'ma give you the understanding to go with it. Just tell me if you heard the word. That's Faith! Faith what I'm talking bout. And if you don't know what I'm talking bout just you listen. Just you think on them old, old people in that itty bitty shack in the woods, them people getting too old to grunt. Them people down in Egypt with the Pharaohs and bitter bread and burdens all the days of they lives. Well, they had Faith. Youall heard bout the mustard seed? That's another story, that's another day. But think on it. Old as they was they ain't never stopped praying and hoping one day a child be born unto them. Yes they did, now. This old Isaac and old Rebecca kept the faith. Asked the Lord for a child to crown they days together and kept the Faith in they hearts one day He would.

Well old Isaac had a master grow watermelons on his farm. And old Isaac he have the best knuckle for miles around for thumping them melons and telling you when they just perfect for the table. He thump and Melon, Mr. Melon, he talk back. Tell his whole life story to that crusty knuckle, Uncle Isaac knock at the door. Yoo-hoo, How you do? Melon say, You a day early, man. Ain't ready yet, Isaac. Got twenty-four hours to go. You traipse on down the patch and find somebody else today. Come back tomorrow I be just right, Brother Isaac.

That was in Africa. Way, way back like I said. Where people talk to animals just like I'm sitting here talking to youall. Don't you go smiling neither. Don't you go signifying and sucking your teeth and raisin your eyebrows and talking bout something you don't know. This old lady got sense just good as any you. Like they say. You got to *Go there to Know there*. And ain't I been sitting on Grandpa's knee hearing him tell bout slavery days and niggers talking to trees and stones and niggers flying like birds. And he was there. He knows. So in

104

a manner of speaking I was there too. He took me back. Heard old Isaac. Rap, rap, rapping. Out there all by hisself in that melon patch and Ole Massa say, Fetch me a good, big one. Got company coming, Isaac. My sister and her no good husband, Isaac, so fetch one the biggest, juiciest. Wouldn't give him the satisfaction of saying he ever got less than the best at my table. So old bent Isaac he down there thumpin and listenin and runnin his fingers long the rind. It's low mo hot too. Even for them old time Georgy niggers it's hot. Isaac so old and dry and tough he don't sweat much anymore but that day down in the patch, water runnin off his hide like it's rainin. He hear Rebecca up in the kitchen. Isaac, Isaac, don't you stay away too long. And he singing back. Got sweaty leg, Got sweaty eye, But this here nigger too old to die. And he picks one with his eye. A long, lean one. Kinda like these people going round here you call em loaf-of-bread head. Long like that. He go over and squat down in the vines and thump it once good with that talking knuckle of his.

Now don't you know that melon crack clean open. Split right dead down the middle just like somebody cleave it with a cane knife. And don't you know there's a baby boy inside. A little chubby-legged, dimple-kneed, brown-eyed boy stuck up in there perfect as two peas in a pod. Yes it was now. A living breathing baby boy hid up in there smiling back at Isaac, grabbing that crusty knuckle and holding on like it was a titty.

Well, old Isaac he sing him a new song now. He's cradling that baby boy and running through the field and singing so fine all the critters got out his way. Rattlesnakes and bears and gators. Nothing was going to mess with Old Isaac on that day. They heard his song and seen the spirit in his eyes, and everything moved on out the way.

And here come old Rebecca, skirts flying, apron flapping in the breeze. Took off fifty years in them twenty-five steps tween the back of that itty bitty cabin and her man's arms. Then they both holding the baby. Both holding and neither one got a hand on him. He just floating in the air between them two old, happy people. Thank the lord. Thank Jesus. Praise his name. They got so happy you coulda built a church right over top them. One of them big, fancy white folks' churches like youall go to nowadays and they so happy they'd of rocked

105

it all by theyselves. Rocked that church and filled it with the
spirit for days, just them two old happy people and that baby
they loved so much didn't even have to hold it. He just floated
on a pillow of air while they praised God.

That's just the way it happened. Isaac found that baby boy
in a watermelon and him and Rebecca had that child they been
praying for every day. It was Faith that bring them that child.
Faith and God's will. Now He couldn't do nothing nice like
that these days. Youall niggers ain't ready. Youall don't believe
in nothing. Old man bring home a baby first thing you do is
call the police or start wagging your tongues and looking for
some young girl under the bed. Youall don't believe nothing.
But the spirit works in mysterious ways his wonders to perform.
Yes He does now. In them old slavery Africa times there was
more miracles in a day than youall gon see in a lifetime. Youall
jumping up and down and ooing and ahhing cause white men
is on the moon and you got shirts you don't have to iron.
Shucks. Some them things Grandpa saw daily scare the spit
out you. And that's just everyday things. Talking to flowers
and rocks and having them answer back. Youall don't believe
in none that. Youall too smarty panted and grown for that. But
old Isaac and Rebecca waited. They kept the faith and that fine
son come to light they last days in this Valley of the Shadows.

Now I could say that's all, I could end it right here. Say
Bread is bread and wine is wine, If anybody asks, this story's
mine. End it happy like that, with a rhyme like the old folks
ended their stories. But there's more. There's the rest goes with
it so I'ma tell it all.

He heard the rest, and it was how the spirit took back the
boy. The rest was the weeping and wailing of old Isaac and
Rebecca. The rest was the broken-hearted despair, the yawning
emptiness of their lives, a hole in their lives even bigger than
the wound they had suffered before the child came. He listened.
He'd never heard such a cruel story before. He was scared. He
was a boy. For all he knew they had found him in a watermelon.
For all he knew he might be snatched back tomorrow. Would
the grown-ups cry for him, would they take to their beds like
old Isaac and Rebecca and wait for death.

May looked round the room catching nobody's eye but
everybody's ear as she finished the rest of her story.

Where was all that praying? Where was all that hallelujah and praise the Lord in that little bitty cabin deep in the woods? I'll tell you where. It was used up. That's where it was. Used up so when trouble came, when night fell wasn't even a match in the house. Nary a pot nor a window. Just two crinkly old people on a shuck mattress shivering under they quilt.

He wanted to forget the rest so he asked if the wino could grow another arm.

May smiled and said God already give him more'n he could use. Arms in his ears, on his toes, arms all over. He just got to figure out how to use what's left.

THE SONGS OF
REBA LOVE JACKSON

The First Song Is for Mama

The first song I'm going to sing is for my mama. My first song
always been dedicated to Mama and always will be long as I'm
drawing breath. Been wearing the white rose in memory of
Mama twenty-five years now. Some of you know what I'm
talking about. Some of you wore mourning white the first time
last Mother's Day Sunday and some been pinning red to they
breast gon be pinning white next time round so my first number
always been for Mama and always will be long as God give
me strength to raise my voice in His praise. Cause that's what
Gospel is. Singing praise to God's name. So I'ma sing a praise
song and dedicate it to the one loved me best on this earth.
The one I loved best and still do. What a Friend. Yes, Lawd.
What a Friend We Have.

One for Brother Harris in Cleveland

When the phone rang so much talking and one another thing
going on didn't nobody stop to answer it you know how you

be busy and everybody think the other person gon get it but
it just keep ringing and might be ringing still if there ain't been
a napkin close to me that don't look used so I wiped the grease
off my fingers and my mouth and picked up the phone.

Hello, hello, I said this the residence of Miss Reba Love
Jackson saying the whole name I don't know why but I said
it all into the phone and didn't get no answer except for some
buzzing at the other end.

Hello, hello again and again I say this Miss Reba Love
Jackson's residence.

Then this voice sorta scratchy and faraway sounding like
it do when it's long distance. I could tell something wrong.
Hear it plain as day in the voice. Poor man talking like he can
hardly keep from crying and what I'm supposed to say? Nobody
but me still ain't paid no tention to the phone. What with folks
eating and talking and somebody at the piano striking off
chords, nobody but me still ain't bothered bout no phone, so
I'm standing there by myself and poor man must of thought
I was Reba Love cause he say his name and commence to
telling me his trouble and I felt so bad standing there I didn't
want to cut the poor man off and I didn't want to hear what
ain't my business to hear but what you going to do?

Finally I had to say wait a minute hold on a minute Sir and
I laid down the receiver and got Reba Love to come. I stood
beside her while she listened. Seems like I could understand
better. Watching how Reba Love listened. How the face of that
saint got sad-eyed while she shook her head from side to side.
I'm hearing the man and understanding him better than when
I was holding the phone my own self. Reba Love nodding like
she do when she sings sometimes but she don't say a word.

Then she sighs and talks in the phone, "Yes yes yes. Surely
I can do that little thing for you. *I Stood on the Bank of Jordan*.
Yes, yes."

And she put her hand over the phone and ask me tell everybody be quiet please. And after some shushing and having to
go around and bodily shut some people up, Reba Love's apart-
ment quiet as church on Monday. She still have her hand over
the mouthpiece and say, "This is my old friend Brother Harris
from Cleveland and he just lost his mama and he needs for me
to sing."

And didn't one more chicken wing crack or ice cube bump round in nobody's Coca-Cola. She raised the receiver like it was a microphone and child I ain't never heard no singing like it. Not Mahalia, not Bessie Griffin, not Sallie Martin. None of them, and I done heard them all, not one coulda touched Reba Love Jackson that evening.

She did it alone at first. The first verse all by herself and the chorus too, just her solo. Then the second verse and she stopped and looked around and whispered into the phone, "I got some good folks here with me and they gon help me sing," whispered it and didn't lose a note, made it all seem like part of what she was singing and believe me when it was time for the rest of us to join in we were *there*, Sister, yes we were now, we were *there*, and Hattie Simpson sat her big self down at the piano too and you better believe Cleveland ain't never heard nothing like it.

For Blind Willie Who Taught Me to Sing

The blind man lay drunk and funky, his feet stretched out on the sidewalk so you had to be careful not to trip over them. Precious Pearl Jackson almost shouted, Look child, look and see the kind of man your daddy is, because she knew somewhere in some city her daughter's no good father would be sleeping off a drunk, probably outdoors like this tramp now that it was summer, snoring like him and like him barefaced and past shame. She didn't say a word but clutched her daughter's hand tighter, tugging her over and past the blind man's filthy lap-tongued brogans.

"Mama, you hurting me."

"You ain't been hurt yet, girl. Just come on here and don't be lagging."

Precious Jackson dreams of different streets. Streets lined with gold and glittering jewels. Streets pure as drifted snow where she can promenade clothed in a milk-white garment whose hem touches the pavements but receives no corruption there. If she had the strength, she would run from her door to the door of the church. People could think she was crazy if they wanted to, but if God granted her the power she would

113

run as fast as the wind down Decatour and across Idlewild and over Frankstown and up the final long block of Homewood, sprinting so her long feet barely touch the ground, clutching her girl to her breast, not breathing till they were safe inside The Sanctified Kingdom of Christ's Holiness Temple. If she could, she would run every step. And it would be like flying. They would not taste of this evil city the Devil had tricked her to, not one swallow of the tainted air. She wondered how it would feel to fly closer to the sun. To have it burn the tacky clothes from her back, and then the skin gone too, all the flesh dropping away like old clothes till the soul rises naked to the Father's side.

Precious Jackson looks down at the gray pavement. She is tall and black and rail thin. Her cropped hair is plastered to her skull by a black net cap. Her round, pop eyes are full and hungry; they burn like the eyes of the saints who never sleep. A sudden breeze drives litter along the high curb and swirls newspapers against the steel gates barricading the shopfronts. Cardboard cartons overflowing with garbage line the curb. Broken glass sparkles in the sunlight. Somebody's crusty, green sock inches down the sidewalk. She knows the blind man. He was a blues singer. Sang the Devil's music in the bars here along the strip. One Saturday night they found him in the Temple. On his knees, they said. Praying in tongues, they said. She remembered him at the mourners' bench. Hunched over on his knees like a man taking a beating. When he arose she expected to see torn and bloody clothing, stripes from the whip. And when he testified it was like reading a book she had sworn to God she would never open. The blind man told it all. She thought the Temple's whitewashed walls would smoke before he finished. So many toils and snares. Listening to the blind man confess his sins, she realized how good her God had been to her. How merciful the straight, hard path He had led her to. Then that mouth of the Devil raised his voice in praise of the Lord. The saints amened his testimony. There was shouting and falling out. The saints offered the hand of Fellowship. The blind man swore by God's grace never to sing blues. Promised to use his voice only to praise God's goodness.

Now he was back in the street again, singing nastiness again. That was him stretched out on the pavement, drunk as sin. She

114

hoped God would snatch his voice as He had snatched his eyes.

The Temple would be visible when they turned the next corner. With its red door as a beacon her eyes would not stray to the fallen city. Precious Pearl envied the people who went to tall churches, churches whose spires could be seen from afar. To be meek and humble, to ask no more than God saw fit to give, to praise affliction because it was a sign of His glorious will, all of this she understood and lived. But she would have liked to worship Him in a cathedral with a mighty organ, and a roof halfway to heaven.

"Come on, gal. Why you lagging this morning?"

Precious Jackson's long feet in flat-heeled shoes slapped the sidewalk. Her daughter was a pitty-pat, pitty-pat keeping up.

"Do you love Jesus?"

"Yes, Mama."

"Do you love Him better than yourself?"

"Yes, Mama."

The words breathless as mother and daughter rushed through the empty, Sunday morning streets. One Sunday in the Temple the blind man sang *Nearer My God to Thee*. Precious Jackson had wept. She had put her arm around her child's stiff, thin shoulders and wept till the song was over.

The sky was a seamless vault of blue. Would it be a sin to paint the ceiling of her church that color. The door, like the door of The Sanctified Kingdom of Christ's Holiness Temple, would be the red of his martyred blood.

A train hooted down by the tracks. Hooted again and Precious Jackson could hear the rattling cars jerked behind it, the sound putting her teeth on edge, then fading, getting soft and white as lamb's wool just before it disappeared. She stopped suddenly and her daughter bumped into her legs. Precious Pearl Jackson felt herself nearly topple. She smacked down where she knew the girl's head would be, her hard head plaited over with cornrows no thicker than scars. Perhaps the world was over. Perhaps everybody was gone. Only the blind blues singer, the girl, and herself, Precious Pearl Jackson, forgotten, left behind. God sweeping the city clean and taking the saints to His bosom in shining silver trains. Perhaps what she had heard was the last load of the blessed taking off for the sun in a beautiful metal bird.

DAMBALLAH

For Old Time Preachin

In those days you could hear real preachin. Not the prancin
and fancy robes and sashayin and jump around like wanta be
Retha Franklin, James Brown or some other kinda rock and
roll superstar with lectronics and guitars and pianos and horns
and ain't never saying a mumblin word what touch the soul.
Real preachin is what I'm talkin about. The man what been
there hisself and when he shout for a witness, witness be fallin
from they seats and runnin down the aisle. Those old time
preachers could tear up a meetin. Tear it up, you hear. And
you talk about talkin. Mmmm. They could do that. Yes indeed.
*E*pistemology and *Cos*mology and *On*tology and *Deu*teronomy.
They was scholars and men and knew the words. Used to be
meetins, what you call revivals today, over in Legion Field
where the white boys played baseball. Peoples drive they trucks
and wagons up here full of chairs just so they can sit in the
outfield cause the bleachers packed every day to hear them
preachers. Real preachin. What you call testimony. Cause the
old timers they knew the world. They knew the world and they
knew the Word and that's why it was real.

I could name you some. I can see them now just as plain
as day. Now I ain't sayin they didn't use showmanship. Had
to do that. Had to draw the people in fore they could whip a
message on em, so they had their ways, yes indeed, a sho nuff
show sometimes. But that be just to get people's tention. You
know what I mean. They had this way of drawin people but
there was more to em than that. Once those brothers got hold
to you they twist and toss and wrestle you like you seen them
little hard-jawed dogs get hold to a rat. And you come out
feelin like you sure enough took some beatin, like somebody
whipped all the black off you and turned you inside out and
ain't nothin ever goin to be the same.

There was one. Prophet Thompson from Talledega. They
had this kinda stage set up at one end the ballpark. Well, you
could see the preachers and the singers comin and goin. Takin
their turns. Now Prophet Thompson he ain't about to walk up
to the platform. Nothing easy like that for him. When his turn
come he rides up on this big, gray, country mule. Yes, he did.

And you ought to heard the shoutin. Prophet ain't said a word yet and they carryin people out the stands. You woulda thought they screamin for the Prophet but all us from the country know those brothers and sisters done got happy behind that lap-eared mule. Mmmp. And the Prophet he knows how to sit a mule. And how to get off one and tie him down so he stays. You woulda believed the place on fire and people burnin up if you heard the tumult and the shoutin from far off. The air be bucklin and them wooden seats rattlin where they stomp they feet and people up off those foldin chairs in the outfield, standin up beatin them funeral parlor chairs like they was tambourines. And the Prophet ain't said nary a word. Just rode in on a mule.

Shoot. That man coulda just rode on out again and left everybody happy. But they was preachers. Real preachers. He knew what to do. That country mule ain't nothin but a trick to get folks' tention. Yes. They knows mules and knows country and the Prophet he just let them have they fun with all that. But when he's on the platform, he knows what to say.

"He brought me up here all the way from the red clay of Talledega, Alabama. So I knows he could get me this little distance to the altar."

And he had to just stand there while the people jump up and down and they clothes fallin like it be raining clothes. Stand there till he ready to say some more, then it's like thunder through the microphone and if he had said *Ground open up and let the spirits of the dead shout too*, nobody been surprised to hear voices comin out that green grass. What he said was, "Some of you all know what I'm talkin about. Some of you know who brought me out of the wilderness and onto this stage in the middle of a darkling plain. Yes Lord. Some of you know the God I speak of, but some of you still thinkin bout old Martin, my mule, and he's good, he's good and faithful, but he ain't nothin but a mule."

You see how he got em. Got em hooked. They don't know whether to run away or stand still. Whether he's talkin to em or about em. Then he commence to preach.

Real preachin. And Prophet Thompson not the onliest one. I could name a many. Seen women throw down mink coats for a preacher to walk on. Seen the aisles lined with furs. First man I ever saw play piano with his feets, it was right here.

117

Back when they used to meet in Legion Field. Preachin and singin like nobody these days knows how to do. I remember seein Reba Love Jackson and her mama, Precious Pearl Jackson, right here every year till her Mama took her away up North. I remember Reba Love in a little baby gown sittin barebottomed in the grass while all that singin goin on, her and the rest of them barebottomed babies and now I see some of them around here gettin bare on top they heads. They say Reba Love's comin back next spring. Won't that be somethin? Won't it though? I heard her Mama dead now. They say Precious Pearl left the Devil down here and died a fine, Christian woman. I knew her well. Let me tell you what I think. Reba Love Jackson be lookin for her Mama when she come back. And you know somethin, God willin she will find her cause this her home. This where it all began. Yes she will. Find her right here and when she does she's gon sing. Sing it. And by The Grace of the Lord I'll live long enough for to see it. To hear that old time singin one more time before I die.

For Somebody Else

Through the windows of the bus Reba Love tries to imagine what it would feel like to be another person. She had heard one of the singers say just a few minutes before, *New Jersey*, and the name of somebody's hometown in the state, so it is night and they are crossing New Jersey and she knows they will stay in a hotel in Newark because the manager knows somebody there who will let them crowd four or five in a room and pay a special rate. She knows many of the gospel groups stay there. She has heard the hotel's name lots of times on the circuit. But nothing out the window is helping her to be someone else. Everything she thinks of, all of the words or voices coming to her will speak only to Reba Love Jackson, speak to her and who she is or will not speak at all. She tries to picture a person she doesn't know. One of the men she can't help seeing when she sings. A man at a concert or in a church who she has never laid eyes on before and probably will not again. The kind of man she is drawn to in spite of herself. A brown man with soft eyes. A man with meat on his bones.

118

Who could laugh with her and grin at the big meals she loves to cook. But this stranger, this unknown, easy man who is not too beautiful, not too young, who does not seem to belong to some hawk-eyed, jealous body else, this stranger who is not really a stranger because she has seen him everywhere and knows she'll see him again, cannot draw her out of herself. This man she has never met, or only met long enough to hear his name before her mother steers him away and returns with some wrinkled, monkey-faced deacon, can not move her from who she is.

She is a Bride of Christ. Sanctified in His service. But there is no mystery here either. What once seemed immense beyond words is as commonplace as cooking and cleaning for a flesh and blood man. Moments of passion surely, surely come, but they are pinpricks of light in the vast darkness which has settled upon her, distant stars which dazzle but do not warm the night sky.

She is not a Bride of Christ. Not since the summer she was thirteen and her mother took her south to visit their People. Seven years away from them and she had just about forgotten her country cousins. Half the people down there seemed to have her last name. Even Tommy Jackson. Little, light-skinned, fast talking T.J. She can't hear him running anymore through the weeds but she can hear T.J.'s holler and the greetings of the others as they bay like bloodhounds over where the picnic cloth is spread under the trees. She is picking up her drawers from the ground. Funny how she was more shamed of her drawers than her bare butt and came out of them so fast she almost scared T.J. away. Once he got his hand up in there she just wanted her underwear gone no matter if she was going to let him do it to her or not. Didn't really seem so important after all. If he did or not. Even after a million warnings and a million threats that this, that or the other thing will happen sure as night follows day or damnation sin, the same old silly stories even after her mother ought to know she knows better. The country girls tell the stories to each other and laugh at them together and mock their mothers telling them. She could never laugh at her mother. Or hurt her any other way. Her mother was a place to stand, a place to lean. Her mama had patched the old underwear so it covered her backside decently.

The patches were a secret, a secret between mother and daughter. And though she could open her legs to T.J., she could not share such secrets.

The grass prickly on her skin when she sat down to pull on her drawers. Sitting because she needed to sit. So the pain and the sweet, warm wetness could run out of her body slowly, on her time, according to her mood instead of the way T.J. had rushed it in. Like he was being chased. Sitting with the Sunday dress still like a wreath around her narrow hips. Suddenly she worried about the wrinkles. Would they fall out? Then she thought about the others girls. Sitting on blankets all day. And the careless ones on grass or even dirt and how all the Sunday dresses will need to be scrubbed and scrubbed. She puts her hand there. The springy hair, the wet and sticky. Her hand. Her fingers like his fingers but his didn't learn anything, didn't stay in one place long enough to let her answer them. Like his fingers only hers are dark like the darkness down there. Her skin night skin like the skin over the windows of the bus. Forever, you could be a thing forever. Or once, one time could change it forever.

She couldn't say no. Couldn't say why she had not said no. So she lied once to her mother and perhaps to God and wore the saints' white dress, the Bridal Dress sanctified and holy in His name.

These things she could not speak of. Like she could not speak of the dead man they found that same day stuck in the roots along the riverbank. The dead man who had been lynched, the grown-ups whispered. When they got him up on shore they sent the children away. Away to play. And she couldn't say no. Couldn't speak about some things. She could only sing them. Put her stories in the songs she had heard all her life so the songs became her stories.

Is there ever any other way she asked herself? Am I to be Reba Love Jackson all the days of my life? Her thoughts are lost in the rumble of the bus. Lights wink and blink and climb the night sky. She is racing across New Jersey in a Greyhound. Could her mother follow the swiftness of her flight? Would her mother be watching all night? Did saints need to sleep? Want to sleep?

She would always be Reba Love Jackson. Till He touched her and brought her on home.

For All Her Fans in Radio Land

......just for voice level could you please say
your full name
>Reba Love Jackson

that's fine, just fine. Now lemme do a little lead-
in: It is my privilege this morning to be talking to Miss Reba
Love Jackson, a great lady who many call the Queen Mother
of Gospel. She is here in our studio on behalf of Watson
Productions who right now at the Uptown Theatre, Sixtieth and
Market, are presenting Miss Reba Love Jackson along with a
host of other stars in the spectacular once-a-year Super Gospel
Caravan. Yes indeed. The Gospel train is stopping here for
three days starting this evening at 7:00 P.M. It's the really big
one youall been waiting for so get down to the Uptown and
pick up on what these soul-stirring folks is all about...that's
enough ... I can fill in later ... Gotta get some other promo
stuff in ... hmmph...but now a Miss a Jackson ... why
don't we start at the beginning...Could you tell our audience
Miss Reba Love Jackson, Gospel Queen, where you were born
>outside Atlanta Georgia in a little
place called Bucolia. Wasn't much to it then and ain't much
to it now. Little country town where everybody one big family
and God the head of the house

I know what you mean. We all know what she
means don't we soul brothers and sisters? Yes siree. Down
home country. We knows all about it, don't we? Fried chicken
and biscuits and grits and the preacher coming over on Sunday
wolfing down half the platter ... Lawd ... Lawd ... Lawd
... but you go on Miss Reba Love Jackson. Tell it like it was.
>we didn't have much. But there was
only my mama and me and we got along. Mama Precious was
a saint. Didn't nobody work harder than my mama worked.
Only heard stories about my father. He died when I was a
baby. Worked on the railroad my mama said and got killed in
an accident. Didn't nobody in Bucolia have much. We children
left school about the age of ten, eleven, and worked in the field
with the grown-ups. Mighty little childhood then. Folks just
didn't have the time they do nowadays to play and get edu-

cation. What I learned I learned from Sunday school and from my mama. But that's the learning stays with you. Cause it's God's truth. Some educated folks . . .

yes. Yes. Educated fools. We all know some like that. But let's go on Miss Reba Love Jackson . . . unlike so many entertainers especially your fellow gospel singers, you've been known for a militant stance in the area of civil rights. Could you tell our audience a little about your involvement in the Movement.

I never did understand no movement, nor no politics, nor nothing like that. People just use my name and put me in that stuff. It's the songs I sing. If you listen those songs tell stories. They got words. And I've always believed in those words. That's why I sing them. And won't sing nothing else. God gave me a little strength and I ain't going to squander it on no Devil's work. We's all God's creatures and it ain't in the Bible to sit in the back of no buses or bow down to any man what ain't nothing but breath and britches. White or black ain't meant to rule God's children. He's the only Master.

right on. Right on, Sister.

Trouble is people don't listen to Gospel music. They pat they feet awhile then they go back on out in them mean streets. They Sunday Christians, so somebody can see them say, Look at Miss Jones in her new hat and new coat. Ain't she something. Go to church to be seen, don't go to hear the Word. That's what keeps the world the crying shame it is. There's a song says, This old world can't last much longer, Reeling and rocking so early in the morning. Another one says, They'll be Peace in the Valley someday. Sure enough, it's gonna come. But it's God trumpet say when. Ain't gon be them white folks telling nobody nothing. Not with their Atom bombs and Hydrogen bombs and naked women and selling people dope and liquor and blowing up little girls in church and dogs and hoses they keep just to hurt people with and every one of them from the President on down full of lies. No. We got to stop bleeding for white people and start leading ourselves in the path of righteousness. He gave His only begotten Son to show the way.

well you sure do tell it like it is . . . now could you say a little about how you got into show business . . . I mean how you rose up to become a household word to millions of your fans.

        wasn't more'n five or six years ago outside of Memphis and we still going around in a raggedy old station wagon. Seven of us singers and no little people in the group. I remember cause Claretta, bless her soul, was sick and we have to stop every half hour or so and that road was hot and dusty and we had three hundred miles to go before we stop for good and had to sing when we got there and Claretta getting worse cause the car had to keep moving. These two cracker state patrols stop us and everybody out they say. And all us womens standing on that highway in the hot sun and these crackers laughing behind they dark glasses and talking about body searches. And talking nastier and nastier. Only thing save us Claretta she ain't said nothing she too scared like the rest of us to say a thing to these nasty patrol but I see her getting all pale like she did when we have to stop the car. Poor child can't hold it no longer and when she start to going right there standing up beside the road and moaning cause she's so ashamed, well that broke it all up and . . .

        yes, mam. I'm sure there are plenty of stories you could tell about the hardships of living in the South

        wasn't only South. You find some of your meanest crackers right here walking the streets of Philadelphia and New York. I been coming this way many a year and let me tell you

        our audience shares your indignation. We know the crosses you had to bear but I bet folks would like to hear how you rose from your humble beginnings to be a star

        God didn't gift me with no fine voice. But he did lay burdens on me and gave me strength to bear them. When I sing people know this. They hear their stories in my songs, that's all

        you're too modest. Miss Reba Love Jackson is an inspiring Christian lady. But they don't call her the Queen of Gospel for nothing. You've got to hear her to believe her. Get on down to the Uptown. Better be there bright and early for a good seat

        I ain't never had the voice of no Mahalia or Willie Mae Ford or none of them . . . but I listened to the best . . . I was raised on the best holy singing ever was. I remember them all coming to Bucolia . . . Kings of Harmony, Selah Jubilee Singers, the Heavenly Gospel Singers from Spartanburg, South Carolina, the Golden Gates, The Hummingbirds and Nightingales and the Mighty Mighty Clouds of Joy . . . and me sitting with my mama listening and thinking if I ever get to Heaven some day please, please, Jesus, let it be like this. Me at my mama's side and angels shaking the roots of the firmament with their voices. The old time people could sing and preach so good it was like they put their hands inside you and just rooted around till they found where you needed to be touched . . . they . . .

I'm sorry to cut you off but our time is running out and our audience wants to hear a little more about what to expect when they catch you at the Uptown . . . I have a piece in my hand written about one of your performances all the way across the pond in Gay Paree. Listen up, youall: "Reba Love Jackson galvanizes the audience . . . No lady on the stage but a roaring black pantheress, leaping, bounding, dancing her songs . . . she embodies what is primitive and powerful in the African soul."

that must be pretty old. Ain't been to Paris, France but once and that was long ago. They tell me I used to get pretty lively when I sang. Kicking up my heels and what not. To tell the truth I never thought much about it. I just sang the old songs and let them take me where they wanted to go. Now I been out here singing a long, long time. Can't hardly remember a time I ain't been out here singing and I'm getting like the fish when the water gets cold. They stop jitterbugging around and sink down to the bottom and lie real still and they be there on the bottom muck alright but you got to go down deep with something special to get them to move.

we'll go on believing what the French soul brother said about you Miss Reba Love Jackson. Our audience can judge for themselves . . . get a taste of that good old time religion when the Super Gospel Caravan pulls into the Uptown tonight. This is one fan who knows he won't be disappointed. I got a feeling Reba Love Jackson, Queen Mother of Gospel, you'll make these clippings seem tame . . . cut.

*   *   *

One for Her Birthday

It is June 19, her birthday and she is sixty-five years old and celebrating by going to the ocean beach for the first time in her life. Atlantic City is like nothing she's ever seen. She is almost giddy in her new slacks suit (her mother never wore pants, not even to work in the fields) sitting it seems a mile above the Boardwalk in a cart driven by a black boy. The intermittently overcast day does not dissipate her spirits. Sheets of fine mist blown up from the water refresh when they daintily sprinkle her face. She had worried at first about her voice. The coarse salt air lodging in her throat and the horror of a cold when she faces the crowd in Convention Hall. But she felt fine. Her voice was a brawny animal still secure at the end of its leash. When she tugged it would be there, and she would turn it loose to do its work at the proper time. She tasted the salt on her tongue. The snapping flags, the striped umbrellas, the bright clothes of the passersby, the giant Ferris wheel blazing with light even in the middle of the afternoon, the calliope disembodied within the roar of the surf, everything she could see, smell, hear, and touch celebrated her birthday.

When the cart arrived at a section of beach littered with dark bodies, she commanded the boy to stop. She hadn't noticed colored bathers elsewhere on the white sand. The boy called back ". . . this Chickenbone Beach, mam," and she understood immediately. This was the place she'd been looking for all along even though she hadn't known it until that moment.

"Wait here please, young man." She was paying him by the hour so she knew he would. She was pleased by his obedience, by the extravagance of it all: a suite in the hotel, a taxi to the boardwalk, a new suit just because she wanted it. People knew her name. Strangers would come up to her on the street and say, You Reba Love, ain't you? Pleased to meet you Miss Reba Love. Leaning against the tubular railing which divided the boardwalk from the beach she rubbed her shoes then the nylon Peds from her feet, exposing wrinkled toes and battered, yellowing toenails. Bad feet. Looked like her mother's long toes splayed down there in the hot sand. Her orange bell-bottoms flap in the stiff breeze. As she marches toward the ocean the soles of her feet squeak with each step. The sand whispers, swishing like the sumptuous robes they wear on stage. Black bodies and ivory bodies and every shade between, halfnaked on the sand.

She thinks of her voice again when the first swirl of icy ocean water laps her toes. Backing away quickly she gasps and hikes up the razor creases of her slacks. Behind her the thumping of bongos and conga drums. In front the restless beard of her Father, a million shades of gray and frothy white. The ocean is too large, too restless. All the dead are out there. Rich and poor, black and white, saints and sinners. And plenty room for the living. Room for those bodies stretched like logs drying in the sun. The wind is furrowing the stiff bristles of her Father's beard, tangling them, caking them with dried spittle and foam as He roars His anger, His loneliness. Depths out there the living will never fill. In the thunder of the surf she can hear newborn babies crying.

The motion of the sea becalms the spinning earth. The breakers unraveling from the horizon freeze to a green shimmer. She wishes she could see His eyes. Eyes which never close and never open. His eyes wherever they are. She wants to see what He sees looking down on her bare head.

A gull shrieks. Then cold shackles draw tighter around her ankles. Holes are opening up in the earth, slowly, subtly, drawing her down. She knows if she does not muster her strength and flee, screaming horses will drag her with them under the waves.

One More Time for Blind Willie

Hate to talk about your mommy she's a good ole soul
She got a buck skin belly and a rubber asshole

Oh Shine, Shine, save poor me
I'll give you more white pussy than you ever did see

Blues verses and toasts and nasty rhymes keep the blind man awake with their spinning and signifying. Voices and voices within voices and half the laughter with him and half at him. The bouncer pitched Blind Willie down the steep, narrow stairs of the speakeasy. Old Willie tumbles out of control. "Told you not to come begging around here bothering the customers." Pitching down so many steps Willie can hear the parts of his body cracking as he falls helpless. So many knife-edged steps Blind Willie has time to fear the horrible impact at the bottom, how his body will be curled into the shape of an egg when he reaches the bottom and the last collision will crack him and scatter him.

> *Stagolee begged Billy,*
> *"Oh please don't take my life.*
> *I got three hungry children*
> *And a very sickly wife."*

First he had believed he was in hell when he awoke to all the moaning and groaning around him. A smell of chemicals in the air. Little teasing voices tormenting him. Then he knew he was still alive because he wasn't burning. He was cold, freezing cold. Colder than he'd ever been. He wished for newspapers to stuff under his clothes. He dreamed of the overcoat he lost in a coon-can game down by the railroad tracks. Heard himself singing about cold hearts and cold women. He was too cold to be dead. He was someplace where white people were talking and laughing.

White hands were peeling away his skin. White eyes lay on him like a blanket of snow. White feet stomped on his chest.

> *Shine, Shine...*

The bouncer and the fall were black. Black hands had pushed him down the endless steps. But the crash, the dying into a thousand pieces are white.

> *Lord ... Help me ... Help me to hold out*

If he could sing now it would be a saint's song. He is on his knees in the Amen Corner of the Temple. He is slamming his fists against the door which even in the darkness throbs red and hot as blood. He smells perfume. Hears a woman's hips, black hips swishing, rubbing against something trying to hold them in. He remembers undressing Carrie May. Pulling down

127

her girdle. The texture of her goosebumpy skin and the rubbery panels. Then how silky she was, how soft with nothing on.

Nearer...

The perfume is a cloud over his head. He is swooning, he is trying to catch his breath, and hold his heart in his chest, and will his belly back down where it belongs so his lungs can fill with air. He is trying to remember the words to a song that gal, Reba Love Jackson sings. She is humming it to help him remember. She is smiling and saying *Come on...Come on in...* to his sweet tenor. They will sing together. One more time.

This Last Song's for Homewood

Whenever I cross these United States of America it does my heart good to stop here and see youall again. Some of you know I got roots here. Deep roots go way back. Lived here in Pittsburgh for a time. Mama worked for some white folks on Winebiddle Street. We lived in Homewood. Many a day I sat waiting for that trolley to bring my mama home. Stopped at Penn and Douglas Avenue and Mama had to walk five blocks to get home. And some of you knows how long five blocks can be after you been scuffling all day in the white people's kitchen. Yes Lawd. Doing all day for them then you got to ride a trolley and foot slog it five blocks and start to cooking and cleaning all over again for your own. It's a long mile. My mama walked it. Yes she did. We all been walking that long mile many a day. You know what I'm talking about. Yes you do, now. Reba Love Jackson ain't always been standing on stage singing praises to the Lawd. I sang His praises down on my knees, youall. *This is my story, This is my song.* Yes. *Praising my Savior. All the day long.* Sang with a scrub brush in my hand. Sometimes I think I ain't never sung no better than I did all by myself on my knees doing daywork in the white folks' kitchen. But I know something about Homewood. In the summertime I'd walk to meet Mama. I'd take her shopping bag and her hand and walk home beside her. I remember every step. Every tree and crack in the pavement from the trolley stop to our little rooms behind Mr. Macks's Grocery. Wasn't a happier little girl in the world than me when I was walking Mama home. Could tell you plenty about Homewood in those days but youall come to hear singing not talking and that's what I'm going to do now. Sing this last one for Homewood. . . .

ACROSS THE
WIDE MISSOURI

THE images are confused now. By time, by necessity. One is Clark Gable brushing his teeth with Scotch, smiling in the mirror because he knows he's doing something cute, grinning because he knows fifty million fans are watching him and also a beautiful lady in whose bathroom and bedroom the plot has him awakening is watching over his shoulder. He is loud and brisk and perfectly at ease cleaning his teeth before such an audience. Like he's been doing that number all his life. And when he turns to face the woman, to greet her, the squeaky clean teeth are part of the smile she devours. This image, the grinning, self-assured man at the sink, the slightly shocked, absolutely charmed woman whose few stray hairs betray the passion of her night with him, a night which was both endless and brief as the time between one camera shot fading and another bursting on the screen, may have been in *Gone With the Wind*, but then again just as likely not. I've forgotten. The image is confused, not clear in itself, nor clearly related to other images, other Rhett Butlers and Scarlett O'Hara's and movies flashing on and off with brief flurries of theme song.

It is spring here in the mountains. The spring which never

133

really arrives at this altitude. Just threatens. Just squats for a
day or a few hours then disappears and makes you suicidal.
The teasing, ultimately withheld spring that is a special season
here and should have its own name. Like Shit. Or Disaster.
Or something of that order. The weather however has nothing
to do with the images. Not the wind or the weather or anything
I can understand forces this handsome man grinning at a mirror
into my consciousness. Nor do geography or climate account
for the inevitable succession—the river, the coins, the song,
the sadness, the recollection—of other images toppling him
and toppling me because it happens no matter where I am, no
matter what the season. In the recollection there is a kind of
unmasking. The white man at the mirror is my father. Then
I know why I am so sad, why the song makes me cry, why
the coins sit where they do, where the river leads.

I am meeting my father. I have written the story before. He
is a waiter in the dining room on the twelfth floor of Kaufman's
Department Store. Not the cafeteria. Be sure you don't get lost
in there. He's in the nicer place where you get served at a
table. The dining room. A red carpet. Ask for him up there if
you get lost. Or ask for Oscar. Mr. Parker. You know Oscar.
He's the headwaiter up there. Oscar who later fell on hard
times or rather hard times fell on him so hard he can't work
anywhere anymore. *Wasn't sickness or nothing else. Just that
whiskey. That's whiskey you see in that corner can't even lift
his head up off the table.* Ask for your daddy, Mr. Lawson,
or ask for Mr. Parker when you get to the twelfth floor. I have
written it before because I hear my mother now, like a person
in a book or a story instructing me. I wrote it that way but it
didn't happen that way because she went with me to Kaufman's. As far as the twelfth floor anyway but she had to pay
an overdue gas bill at the gas company office and ride the
trolley back to Homewood and she had to see Dr. Barnhart and
wanted to be home when I got there. The whole idea of meeting
my father for lunch and a movie was hers and part of her idea
was just the two of us, Daddy and me, alone. So my mother
pointed to the large, red-carpeted room and I remember wanting
to kiss her, to wait with her at the elevators after she pushed
the button and the green arrow pointed down. If I had written
it that way the first time I would be kissing her again and

smelling her perfume and hearing the bells and steel pulleys of the elevators and staring again apprehensively through the back of my head at the cavernous room full of white people and the black men in white coats moving silently as ghosts but none of them my father.

The entrance way to the restaurant must have been wide. The way overpriced restaurants are with the cash register off to one side and aisles made by the sides of high-backed booths. Wide but cordoned by a rope, a gold-braided, perhaps tasseled rope, stretched between brass, waist-high poles whose round, fluted bases could slide easily anywhere along the red carpet. A large white woman in a silky, floral patterned dress is standing like she always does beside the pole, and the gold rope swallows its own tail when she loops both ends into a hook at the top of one of the poles.

I must have said then to myself *I am meeting my father.* Said that to myself and to the woman's eyes which seemed both not to see me and to stare so deeply inside me I cringed in shame. In my shyness and nervousness and downright fear I must have talked a lot to myself. Outside the judge's chambers in the marble halls of the courthouse, years later waiting to plead for my brother, I felt the same intimidation, the same need to remind myself that I had a right to be where I was. That the messages coded into the walls and doors and ceilings and floors, into the substances of which they were made, could be confronted, that I could talk and breathe in the storm of words flung at me by the invisible architects who had disciplined the space in which I found myself.

Daddy. Daddy. I am outside his door in the morning. His snores fill the tiny room. More a storage closet than room, separated from the rest of the house so the furnace doesn't heat it. The bed is small but it touches three walls. His *door* is actually a curtain hanging from a string. We live on the second floor so I am out in the hall, on a landing above the icy stairwell calling to him. *Your father worked late last night. Youall better be quiet this morning so he can get some sleep*, but I am there, on the cold linoleum listening to him snore, smelling his sleep, the man smell I wonder now if I've inherited so it trails me, and stamps my things mine when my kids are messing around where they shouldn't be. I am talking to myself when he stirs in that darkness behind the curtain. He groans and the mattress groans under him and the green metal cot squeaks as he shifts to another place in his dreaming.

I say to myself, *Where is he?* I stare at all the black faces. They won't stay still. Bobbing and bowing into the white faces or gliding toward the far swinging doors, the closely cropped heads poised and impenetrable above mandarin collars. Toomer called the white faces petals of dusk and I think now of the waiters insinuating themselves like birds into clusters of petals, dipping silently, silently depositing pollen or whatever makes flowers grow and white people be nice to black people. And tips bloom. I am seeing it in slow motion now, the courtship, the petals, the starched white coats elegant as sails plying the red sea. In my story it is noise and a blur of images. Dark faces never still long enough to be my father.

"Hey, Eddie, look who's here."

There is a white cloth on the table that nearly hangs to the floor. My knees are lost beneath it, it's heavy as a blanket, but Oscar has another white cloth draped over his arm and unfurls it so it pops like a flag or a shoeshine rag and spreads it on top of the other so the table is covered twice. When Oscar sat me down, two cups and saucers were on the table. He went to get my father and told me he'd be right back and fix me up and wasn't I getting big and looked just like my daddy. He had scraped a few crumbs from the edge of the table into his hand and grinned across the miles of white cloth at me and the cups and saucers. While he was gone I had nudged the saucer to see if it was as heavy as it looked. Under the edge closest to me were three dimes. Two shiny ones and one yellow as a bad tooth. I pushed some more and found other coins, two fat quarters neither new nor worn. So there I was at that huge table and all that money in front of me but too scared to touch it so I slid the ten-pound cup and saucer back over the coins and tried to figure out what to do. Knew I better not touch the table cloth. Knew I couldn't help spotting it or smudging it if my hand actually touched the whiteness. So I tried to shove the money with the base of the saucer, work it over to the end of the table so it'd drop in my hand, but I couldn't see what I was doing and the cup rattled and I could just see that little bit of coffee in the bottom come jumping up out the cup and me worried that whoever had forgotten the quarters and dimes would remember and surely come back for them then what would I say would I lie and they'd know a little nigger at a big snow white table like this had to be lying, what else I'm gonna do but lie and everybody in the place know the thief had to be me and I was thinking and worrying and wondering what my father would do if all those people came after me and by that time I just went on and snatched that money and catch me if you can.

"Look who's here, Eddie." And under my breath I said shut up Mr. Oscar Parker, keep quiet man you must want everybody in here listening to those coins rattling in my pocket. Rattling loud as a rattlesnake and about to bite my leg through my new pants. Go on about your business, man. Look who ain't here. Ain't nobody here so why don't you go on away.

Then my father picked up the saucers and balled up the old top cloth in one hand, his long fingers gobbling it and tucking it under his arm. Oscar popped the new one like a shoeshine rag and spread it down over the table. Laid it down quiet and soft as new snow.

"Busboy'll git you a place setting. Eddie, you want one?"

"No. I'll just sit with him."

"Sure looks like his daddy."

"Guess he ought to."

"Guess he better."

I don't remember what I ate. I don't recall anything my father said to me. When I wrote this before there was dialogue. A lot of conversation broken by stage directions and the intrusions of restaurant business and restaurant noise. Father and son an island in the midst of a red-carpeted chaos of white people and black waiters and the city lurking in the wings to swallow them both when they take the elevator to the ground floor and pass through Kaufman's green glass revolving doors. But it didn't happen that way. We did talk. As much as we ever did. Both of us awkward and constrained as we still are when we try to talk. I forget all the words. Words were unimportant because what counted was his presence, talking or silent didn't matter. Point was he was with me and would stay with me the whole afternoon. One thing he must have asked me about was the movies. I believe I knew what was playing at every theater downtown and knew the address of every one and could have reeled off for him the names of the stars and

137

what the ads said about each one. The images are not clear but I still can see the way the movie page was laid out. I had it all memorized but when he asked me I didn't recite what I knew, didn't even state a preference because I didn't care. Going with him was what mattered. Going together, wherever, was enough. So I waited for him at the table. Wondering what I had eaten, running my tongue around in my mouth to see if I could get a clue. Because the food had been served and I had wolfed it down but he was all I tasted. His presence my feast.

He came back without the white coat. He brought a newspaper with him and read to himself a minute then read me bits and pieces of what I knew was there. Him reading changed it all. He knew things I had never even guessed at when I read the movie page the night before. Why one show was jive, why another would be a waste of money, how long it would take to walk to some, how others were too far away. I wanted to tell him it didn't matter, that one was just as good as another, but I didn't open my mouth till I heard in his voice the one he wanted to see.

He is six foot tall. His skin is deep brown with Indian red in it. My mother has a strip of pictures taken in a five and dime, taken probably by the machine that was still in Murphy's 5&10 when Murphy's was still on Homewood Avenue when I was little. Or maybe in one of the booths at Kennywood Amusement Park which are still there. They are teenagers in the picture, grinning at the automatic camera they've fed a quarter. Mom looks pale, washed out, all the color stolen from her face by the popping flashbulbs. His face in the black and white snapshots is darker than it really is. Black as Sambo if you want to get him mad you can say that. Black as Little Black Sambo. Four black-as-coal spots on the strip. But if you look closely you see how handsome he was then. Smiling his way through four successive poses. Each time a little closer to my mother's face, tilting her way and probably busy with his hands off camera because by picture three that solemn grandmother look is breaking up and by the final shot she too is grinning. You see his big, heavy-lidded, long-lashed, theatrical eyes. You see the teeth flashing in his wide mouth and the consciousness, lacking all self-consciousness and vanity, of how good he looks. Black, or rather purple now that the photos have faded, but if you get past the lie of the color he is clearly one of those *brown-eyed, handsome men* people like Chuck Berry sing about and other people lynch.

"Here's a good one. Meant to look at the paper before now, but we been real busy. Wanted to be sure there was a good one but it's alright, got a Western at the Stanley and it's just down a couple blocks past Gimbels. Clark Gable's in it. *Across the Wide Missouri*."

The song goes something like this: *A white man loved an Indian Maiden* and la de da–/–la de da. And: *A–way, you've gone away...Across the wide Mis–sour–i*. Or at least those words are in it, I think. I think I don't know the words on purpose. For the same reason I don't have it on a record. Maybe fifteen or twenty times in the thirty years since I saw the movie I've heard the song or pieces of the song again. Each time I want to cry. Or do cry silently to myself. A flood of tears the iron color of the wide Missouri I remember from the movie. *A–way, we're gone a–way...Across the wide Missouri*. It's enough to have it in pieces. It's enough to have heard it once and then never again all the way through but just in fragments. Like a spring which never comes. But you see a few flowers burst open. And a black cloud move down a grassy slope. A robin. Long, fine legs in a pair of shorts. The sun hot on your face if you lie down out of the wind. The fits and starts and rhythms and phrases from the spring-not-coming which is the source of all springs that do come.

The last time I heard the song my son called it *Shenandoah*. Maybe that's what it should be called. Again I don't know. It's something a very strong instinct has told me to leave alone. To take what comes but don't try to make anything more out of it than is there. In the fragments. The bits and pieces. The coincidences like hearing my son hum the song and asking him about it and finding out his class learned it in school and will sing it on Song Night when the second grade of Slade School performs for their parents. He knew the words of a few verses and I asked him to sing them. He seemed pleased that I asked and chirped away in a slightly cracked, slightly breathless, sweet, second grade boy's voice.

Now I realize I missed the concert. Had a choice between Song Night and entertaining a visiting poet who had won a Pulitzer Prize. I chose—without even remembering *Across the Wide Missouri*—the night of too many drinks at dinner and too

139

much wine and too much fretting within skins of words and too much, too much until the bar closed and identities had been defrocked and we were all clichés, as cliché as the syrupy Shenandoah, stumbling through the swinging doors out into Laramie's cold and wind.

I will ask my son to sing it again. I hope he remembers the words. Perhaps I'll cheat and learn a verse myself so I can say the lyrics rather than mumble along with the tune when it comes into my head. Perhaps I'll find a way to talk to my father. About things like his presence. Like taking me to the movies once, alone, just the two of us in a downtown theater and seeing him for the whole ninety minutes doing good and being brave and handsome and thundering like a god across the screen. Or brushing his teeth loudly in the morning at the sink. Because I understand a little better now why it happened so seldom. (Once?) It couldn't have been only once in all those years. The once is symbolic. It's an image. It's a blurring of reality the way certain shots in a film blur or distort in order to focus. I understand better now the river, the coins, the song, the sadness, the recollection. I have sons now. I've been with them often to the movies. Because the nature of my work is different from my father's. I am freer. I have more time and money. He must have been doing some things right or I wouldn't have made it. Couldn't have. He laughed when I told him years later about "finding" money on the table. I had been a waiter by then. In Atlantic City during summer vacations from school at the Morton Hotel on the Boardwalk. I knew about tips. About some people's manners and propriety. Why some people treat their money like feces and have a compulsion to conceal it, hide it in all sorts of strange places. Like under the edge of saucers. Like they're ashamed or like they get off playing hide and seek. Or maybe just have picked up a habit from their fathers. Anyway he laughed when I told him and said Oscar probably damned a couple of poor little old white ladies to hell for not leaving him a tip. Laughed and said, *They're probably burning in hell behind you "finding" that money.*

I understand a little more now. Not much. I have sons of my own and my father has grandsons and is still a handsome man. But I don't see him often. And sometimes the grandson who has his name as a middle name, the one who can say

Shenandoah if he wants to call it that, doesn't even remember who his grandfather is. *Oh yeah*, he'll say. *Edgar in Pittsburgh*, he'll say. *Your father. Yeah. I remember now.*

But he forgets lots of things. He's the kind of kid who forgets lots of things but who remembers everything. He has the gift of feeling. Things don't touch him, they imprint. You can see it sometimes. And it hurts. He already knows he will suffer for whatever he knows. Maybe that's why he forgets so much.

RASHAD

▄▲▄▲▄▲▄▲▄▲▄▲▄▲▄▲▄▲▄▲▄▲▄▲▄▲▄▲

Rashad's home again. Nigger's clean and lean and driving a mean machine. They say he's dealing now, dealing big in the Big D, Deetroit. Rashad's into something, sure nuff. The cat's pushing a silver Regal and got silver threads to match. Yea, he's home again. Clean as he wants to be. That suit ain't off nobody's rack. One of a kind. New as a baby's behind. Driving a customized Regal with RASHAD on the plate.

IT was time for it to go, all of it. Nail and banner both. Time she said as she eased out the nail on which it hung. Past time she thought as she wiggled the nail and plaster trickled behind the banner, spattering the wall, sprinkling the bare floorboards in back of the chair where the rug didn't reach. Like cheese, she thought. All these old walls like rotten cheese. That's why she kept everybody's pictures on the mantelpiece. Crowded as it was now with photos of children and grandchildren and nephews and nieces and the brown oval-framed portraits of people already old when she was just a child, crowded as it was there was no place else to put the pictures of the people she loved because the rotten plaster wouldn't take a nail.

The banner was dry and crinkly. Like a veil as she rolled it in her hands, the black veils on the little black hats her mother had worn to church. The women of Homewood A.M.E. Zion used to keep their heads covered in church. Some like her Grandmother Gert and Aunt Aida even hid their faces behind crinkly, black veils. She rolled the banner tighter. Its backside was dusty, an arc of mildew like whitish ash stained the dark cylinder she gripped in both hands. How long had the banner been hanging in the corner. How long had she been in this house on Finance street? How long had the Homewood streets been filling with snow in the winter and leaves in fall and the cries of her children playing in the sunshine? How long since she'd driven in the nail and slipped the gold-tasseled cord over it so the banner hung straight? No way to make the banner stand up on the mantelpiece with the photos so she'd pounded a nail into the wall behind the overstuffed chair cursing as she had heard the insides of the rotten wall crumbling, praying with each blow of the hammer the nail would catch something solid and hold. Because embroidered in the black silk banner was the likeness of her granddaughter Keesha, her daughter's first baby, and the snapshot from which the likeness on the banner had been made, the only photo anybody had of the baby, was six thousand miles away in her daddy's wallet.

Rashad had taken the picture with him to Vietnam. She had given it up grudgingly. Just before he left, Rashad had come to her wanting to make peace. He looked better than he had in months. I'm clean, Mom. I'm OK now, he'd said. He called her mom and sometimes she liked it and sometimes it made her blood boil. Just because he'd married her daughter, just because there'd been nobody when he was growing up he could call mom, just because he thought he was cute and thought she was such a melon head he could get on her good side by sweet talking and batting his droopy eyelashes and calling her mom, just because of all that, and six thousand miles and a jungle where black boys were dying like flies, just because of all that, if he thought she was going to put the only picture of her granddaughter in his hot, grabby, long-fingered hand, he better think again. But he had knocked at her door wanting to talk peace. Peace was in him the way he'd sat and crossed one leg over his knee, the way he'd cut down that wild bush growing out the top of his head, and trimmed his moustache and shaved the scraggly goat beard, peace was in his hands clasped atop his knees and in the way he leaned toward her and talked soft. I know I been wrong, Mom. Nobody knows better than me how wrong I been. That stuff makes you sick. It's like you ain't yourself. That monkey gets you and you don't care nothing about nobody. But I'm OK now. I ain't sick now. I'm clean. I love my wife and love my baby and I'ma do right now, Mom.

So when he asked she had made peace too. Like a fool she

almost cried when she went to the mantelpiece and pulled out the snapshot from the corner of the cardboard frame of Shirley's prom picture. She had had plans for the photo of her granddaughter. A silver frame from the window of the jewelry shop she passed every morning on her way to work. But she freed it from the top corner of the cardboard border where she had tucked it, where it didn't cover anything but the fronds of the fake palm tree behind Shirley and her tuxedoed beau, where it could stay and be seen till she got the money together for the silver frame, freed the snapshot and handed it to her granddaughter's daddy, Rashad, to seal the peace.

Then one day the package came in the mail. The postman rang and she was late as usual for work and missed her bus standing there signing for it and he was mad too because she had kept him waiting while she pulled a housecoat over her slip and buttoned it and tied a scarf around her head.

Sign right there. Right there where it says received by. Right there, lady. And she cut her eyes at him as if to say I don't care how much mail you got in that sack don't be rushing me you already made me miss my bus and I ain't hardly answering my door half naked.

I can read, thank you. And signs her name letter by letter as if maybe she can read but maybe she had forgotten how to write. Taking her own good time because his pounding on the door again after she hollered out, Just a minute, didn't hurry her but slowed her down like maybe she didn't quite know how to button a housecoat or wrap her uncombed hair in a scarf and she took her time remembering.

Thank you when she snatched the package and shut the door louder than she needed to. Not slamming it in the mailman's face but loud enough to let him know he wasn't the only one with business in the morning.

Inside, wrapped in pounds of tissue paper, was the banner. At first she didn't know what it was. She stared again at the rows of brightly colored stamps on the outside of the brown paper. Rashad's name and number were in one corner, "Shirley and Mom" printed with the same little-boy purple crayon letters across the middle of the wrapping paper. Handfuls of white tissue inside a grayish box. Then the black silk banner with colored threads weaving a design into the material. She didn't know what it was at first. She held it in her fingertips at arm's

length, righting it, letting it unfurl. It couldn't be a little fancy
China doll dress Rashad had sent from overseas for Keesha,
she knew that, but that's what she thought of first, letting it
dangle there in her outstretched arms, turning it, thinking of
how she'll have to iron out the wrinkles and be careful not to
let her evil iron get too hot.

Then she recognized a child's face. Puffy-cheeked, smiling,
with curly black hair and slightly slanting black eyes, the face
of a baby like they have over there in the jungle where Rashad's
fighting. A pretty picture with a tiny snowcapped mountain
and blue lake worked into the background with the same luminous threads which raise the child's face above the sea of
black silk. Though the baby's mouth is curled into a smile and
the little mountain scene floating in the background is prettier
than anyplace she has ever been, the banner is sad. It's not the
deep creases she will have to iron out or the wrinkles it picked
up lying in its bed of tissue paper. It's the face, something sad
and familiar in the face. She saw her daughter's eyes, Shirley's
eyes dripping sadness the way they were in the middle of the
night that first time she ran home from Rashad. Pounding at
the door. Shirley standing there shaking on the dark porch.
Like she might run away again into the night or collapse there
in the doorway where she stood trembling in her tracks. He hit
me. He hit me, Mama. Shirley in her arms, little girl shudders.
You can't fight him. He's a man, baby. You can't fight him
like you're another man.

Shirley's eyes in the baby's face. They used to tease her,
call Shirley *Chink* because she had that pale yellowish skin and
big eyes that seemed turned up at the corners. Then she remembered the picture she had sent away with Rashad. She read
the word in the bottom corner of the banner which had been
staring at her all this time, the strip of green letters she had
taken for part of the design till she saw her daughter's eyes in
the baby face and looked closer and read *Keesha*.

How many years now had they been teasing Keesha about
that picture hanging in the corner of the living room?

Take it down, Grammy. Please take that ugly thing down.

Can't do that, baby. It's you, baby. It's something special
your daddy had made for you.

It's ugly. Don't look nothing like me.

Your daddy paid lots of money for that picture. Someday you'll appreciate it.

Won't never like nothing that ugly. I ain't no chinky-chinky Chinaman. That's what they always be teasing me about. I ain't no chinky baby.

How many years had the banner been there behind the big spaghetti gut chair in the dark corner of her living room? The war was over now. Rashad and the rest of the boys back home again. How long ago had a little yellow man in those black pajamas like they all wear over there held her granddaughter's picture in his little monkey hand and grinned at it and grinned at Rashad and taken the money and started weaving the face in the cloth. He's probably dead now. Probably long gone like so many of them over there they bombed and shot and burned with that gasoline they shot from airplanes. A sad, little old man. Maybe they killed his granddaughter. Maybe he took Rashad's money and put his own little girl's face on the silk. Maybe it's the dead girl he was seeing even with Keesha's picture right there beside him while he's sewing. Maybe that's the sadness she saw when she opened the package and saw again and again till she learned never to look in that corner above the mush springed chair.

Keesha had to be eleven now, with her long colty legs and high, round, muscley butt. Boys calling her on the phone already. Already getting blood in her cheeks if you say the right little boy's name. Keesha getting grown now and her sister Tammy right behind her. Growing up even faster cause she's afraid her big sister got a head start and she ain't never gonna catch up. That's right. That's how it's always gon be. You'll have to watch that child like a hawk. You think Keesha was fast? Lemme tell you something. You'll be wishing it was still Keesha you chasing when that Tammy goes flying by.

They get to that certain age and you can't tell them nothing. No indeed. You can talk till you're blue in the face and they ain't heard a word. That's the way you were, Miss Ann. Don't be cutting your big China eyes at me because that's just the way you were. Talked myself blue in the face but it was Rashad this and Rashad that and I mize well be talking to myself because you were gonna have him if it killed you.

She unrolls the banner to make sure she didn't pull it too

149

tight. It's still there, the bright threads still intact, the sad, dead child smiling up at her. The dead child across the ocean, her dead granddaughter Kaleesha, her own stillborn son. When you looked at it closely you could see how thicker, colored threads were fastened to the silk with hundreds of barely visible black stitches. Thinner than spider's web the strands of black looped around the cords of gold and bronze and silver which gave the baby's face its mottled, luminous sheen. From a distance the colors and textures of the portrait blended but up close the child's face was a patchwork of glowing scars, as ugly as Keesha said it was. Rashad had paid good money for it sure enough but if the old man had wept when he made it, there must have been times when he laughed too. A slick old yellow man, a sly old dog taking all that good money and laughing cause it didn't matter whose face he stuck on that rag.

She had heard Rashad talk about the war. One of those nights when Shirley had run back home to Mama he had followed her and climbed through a basement window and fallen asleep downstairs in the living room. She heard him before she saw him stretched out on her couch, his stingy brim tipped down over his eyes, his long, knobby-toed shoes propped up on the arm of the couch. His snores filled the room. She had paused on the steps, frightened by the strange rumbling noise till she figured out what it had to be. Standing above him in the darkness she'd wanted to smack his long shoes, knock the hat off his nose. He's the one. This is the nigger messing over my little girl. This the so-called man whipping on my baby. She thought of her sons, how she had to beg, how she just about had to get down on her knees and plead with them not to go to their sister's house and break this scrawny nigger's neck.

He's sick, Mama. He can't help it. He loves me and loves the baby. He came back sick from that filthy war. They made him sick again over there.

She looked down at Rashad sleeping on her couch. Even with the trench coat draped over his body she could see how thin he was. Skin and bones. Junkie thin because they just eat sugar, don't want nothing but sugar, it's all they crave when that poison gets hold to them. Her sons wanted to kill him and would have if she hadn't begged them on her knees.

150

She has to fight her own battles. Your sister's a grown woman. Stay away from there, please.

She had felt the darkness that night, heavy as wind swirling around her. She had come downstairs for a glass of wine, the sweet Mogen David in the refrigerator which once or twice a month would put her to sleep when nothing else would. She had a headache and her heart had been pounding ever since she opened the door and saw Shirley with Keesha in her arms standing on the porch. There had been calls earlier in the evening, and Keesha howling in the background and Shirley sobbing the second time and then it was midnight and what was she going to do, what could she say this time when the baby was finally asleep and the coffee cups were empty and there were just the two of them, two women alone in the middle of the night in that bright kitchen. Finally Shirley asleep too but then her stomach and her pounding heart turned her out of bed and she checked Shirley and the baby again and tipped down the steps needing that glass of wine to do the trick and there he was, the sound of his snoring before she saw him and then the night swirling like a wind so she was driven a thousand miles away from him, from his frail, dope-smelling bones under that raggedy trench coat, a thousand miles from him and anyone, anything alive.

It was his screaming which broke her sleep again, the last time that night or morning because one had bled into the other and she heard him yell like a man on fire and heard Shirley flying down the stairs and by the time she got herself together and into her robe and downstairs into the living room, Shirley was with him under the trench coat and both were quiet as if no scream had clawed sleep from her eyes and no terror had nearly ripped his skinny body apart.

Sunday morning then, too late and too tired to go to church then so it was the three of them at the table drinking coffee and nodding with that burden of no sleep from the night before, Shirley, Rashad, her own weary self at the table when he talked about the war.

I was a cook. Had me a good job. You know. Something keeps your butt away from the killing. A good job cause you could do a little business. Like, you know. A little hustle on the side. Like be dealing something besides beans to them crazy

151

niggers. Little weed, little smack. You get it from the same
gooks sold you the salt and pepper. Had me a nice little hustle
going. Been alright too cept some brothers always got to be
greedy. Always got to have it all. Motherfucker gon gorilla me
and take my little piece of action. Say he's the man and I'm
cutting in on his business. Well one thing led to another. Went
down on the dude. Showed him he wasn't messing with no
punk. Eyes like to pop out his head when I put my iron in his
belly. You know like I thought that was that and the nigger
was gon leave me alone but he set me up. Him and some of
them jive MPs he's paying off they set me up good and I got
busted and sent home. Still be in jail if I hadn't copped a plea
on possession and took my dishonorable.

Yeah, they be killing and burning and fragging and all that
mess but I only heard stories about it, I had me a good job,
I was feeding niggers and getting niggers high. Getting them
fat for the jungle. And getting my ownself as messed up as
you see me now, sitting here at this table not worth a good
gcddamn to nobody.

She knew there was more to tell. She knew he had been in
bad fighting once because her daughter was always reading the
newspapers and calling her on the phone and crying and saying,
He's dead, Mama. I know he's dead and my poor little girl
won't never know her daddy. That was before his good job,
before the dope he said was as easy to get as turning on a
faucet. But he wouldn't talk about the fighting. He'd dream
about the fighting and wake up screaming in the night but he
wouldn't talk.

Now she had it down, rolled in her hands, and had to put
the banner someplace. It was time to take it down, she knew
that but didn't know where to put it now it was off her wall.
Where the nail had been, a dug-out, crumbly looking hole
gaped in the plaster. If she touched it, the rotten wall might
crack from floor to ceiling, the whole house come tumbling
down around her heels. A knuckle-sized chunk of wall gone
but she could fix it with patching plaster and in the dark corner
nobody would hardly notice. The paint had sweated badly over
the chair and a stain spread across the ceiling over the corner
so one more little spot a different color than the rest wouldn't
matter because the rest wasn't one color, the rest was leaks and

patches and coming apart and faded and as tired of standing as she was tired of holding it up.

One day she'd like to tear the walls down. Go round with a hammer and knock them all down. She knew how the hammer would feel in her fist, she knew how good each blow would feel and she could hear herself shouting hallelujah getting it done.

But she needed someplace to put the banner. She was late as usual and Shirley and the girls would be by soon to go to church. Shirley might be driving Rashad's new car. On Sunday morning he sure wouldn't be needing it. Be dinnertime before he was up and around so he might give Shirley the keys so she could drive the girls to church in style. The girls loved their daddy and he loved them. When he came to town it was always a holiday for the girls. Presents and rides and money and a pretty daddy to brag on for months till he appeared again. She wondered how long it would be this time. How long he'd be flying high before somebody shot him or the police caught up with him and then he'd be dead or in jail again and he'd fall in love again with "Shirley and Mom."

Here she was with the banner still in her hand and the kitchen clock saying late, you're late woman and she's still in her robe, hasn't even filled the tub yet but she just had to stop what she was supposed to be doing and take it down. Well, when the girls come knocking at the door, calling and giggling and signifying and Shirley sits behind the wheel honking to rush her, she'll fling open the door and stuff it in their hands. It will be gone then. Someplace else then, because she never really wanted that sad thing in the first place. She didn't understand why she'd left it hanging this long, why she let it move in and take over that dark corner behind the chair. Because it was a sad thing. A picture of somebody wasn't ever in the family. More of Rashad's foolishness. Spending money when he has it like money's going out of style. Rashad living like a king and throwing a handful of money at the old yellow man when the banner is finished. Rashad living fast because he knows he's gonna die fast and the old chink grinning up at the black fool, raking in the dollars Rashad just threw on the floor like he got barrels of money, stacks of money and don't know how to give it away fast enough.

She loves him too. That handful of money he throws over his shoulder would feel like the hammer in her hand. She'll pray for Rashad today. And Tommy. So much alike. A long hard prayer and it will be like hoisting the red bricks of Homewood A.M.E. Zion on her shoulders and trying to lift the whole building or trying to lift all of Homewood. The trees and houses and sidewalks and all the shiny cars parked at the curb. It will be that hard to pray them home, to make them safe.

She starts up the stairs with the rolled banner still in her hand. She'll soak a little in the tub even if it makes her later. They can wait awhile. Won't hurt them to wait a little while. She's been waiting for them all the days of her life and they can just sit tight awhile because she needs to pray for them too. Pray for all of them and needs all her strength so she'll soak in the tub awhile.

At the top of the steps, at the place they turn and her sons have to stoop to get by without bumping their heads on the low ceiling, at that turning where she always stoops too, not because her head would hit if she didn't but because the slight bend forward of her body brings them back, returns her sons to this house where they all grew tall, taller than the ceiling so they had to stoop to get past the turning, at that place near the top of the stairs when she stoops and they are inside her again, babies again, she thinks of the old man sewing in his hut no bigger than a doghouse.

Rashad would lean in and hand him the photo. The peace offering she sent with him all those miles across the ocean. The old man would take the snapshot and look at it and nod when Rashad pointed to the banners and faces hanging in the hut. A little wrinkled old man. A bent old man whose fingers pained him like hers did in the morning. Swollen fingers and crooked joints. Hands like somebody been beating them with a hammer. She had kept it hanging this long because he had sewn it with those crippled fingers. She took it down because the old man was tired, because it was time to rest, because Keesha was almost grown now and her face was with the others decorating the mantel.

She saw him clearly at that turning of the stairs and understood the sadness in the eyes. The lost child she would pray for too.

TOMMY

He checks out the Velvet Slipper. Can't see shit for a minute in the darkness. Just the jukebox and beer smell and the stink from the men's room door always hanging open. Carl ain't there yet. Must be his methadone day. Carl with his bad feet like he's in slow motion wants to lay them dogs down easy as he can on the hot sidewalk. Little sissy walking on eggs steps pussy-footing up Frankstown to the clinic. Uncle Carl ain't treating to no beer to start the day so he backs out into the brightness of the Avenue, to the early afternoon street quiet after the blast of nigger music and nigger talk.

Ain't nothing to it. Nothing. If he goes left under the trestle and up the stone steps or ducks up the bare path worn through the weeds on the hillside he can walk along the tracks to the park. Early for the park. The sun everywhere now giving the grass a yellow sheen. If he goes right it's down the Avenue to where the supermarkets and the 5&10 used to be. Man, they sure did fuck with this place. What he thinks each time he stares at what was once the heart of Homewood. Nothing. A parking lot and empty parking stalls with busted meters. Only a fool leave his car next to one of the bent meter poles. Places to park so you can shop in stores that ain't there no more. Remembers his little Saturday morning wagon hustle when him and all the other kids would lay outside the A&P to haul groceries. Still some white ladies in those days come down from Thomas Boulevard to shop and if you're lucky get one of them and get tipped a quarter. Some of them fat black bitches be in church every Sunday have you pulling ten tons of rice and beans all the way to West Hell and be smiling and yakking all the way and saying what a nice boy you are and I knowed your mama when she was little and please sonny just set them inside on the table and still be smiling at you with some warm glass of water and a dime after you done hauled their shit halfway round the world.

Hot in the street but nobody didn't like you just coming in and sitting in their air conditioning unless you gonna buy a drink and set it in front of you. The poolroom hot. And too early to be messing with those fools on the corner. Always somebody trying to hustle. Man, when you gonna give me my money, Man, I been waiting too long for my money, Man, lemme hold this quarter till tonight, Man. I'm getting over tonight, Man. And the buses climbing the hill and turning the corner by the state store and fools parked in the middle of the street and niggers getting hot honking to get by and niggers paying them no mind like they got important business and just gonna sit there blocking traffic as long as they please and the buses growling and farting those fumes when they struggle around the corner.

Look to the right and to the left but ain't nothing to it, nothing saying move one way or the other. Homewood Avenue a darker gray stripe between the gray sidewalks. Tar patches in the asphalt. Looks like somebody's bad head with the ringworm. Along the curb ground glass sparkles below the broken neck of a Tokay bottle. Just the long neck and shoulders of the bottle intact and a piece of label hanging. Somebody should make a deep ditch out of Homewood Avenue and just go on and push the row houses and boarded storefronts into the hole. Bury it all, like in a movie he had seen a dam burst and the flood waters ripping through the dry bed of a river till the roaring water overflowed the banks and swept away trees and houses, uprooting everything in its path like a cleansing wind.

He sees Homewood Avenue dipping and twisting at Hamilton. Where Homewood crests at Frankstown the heat is a shimmering curtain above the trolley tracks. No trolleys anymore. But the slippery tracks still embedded in the asphalt streets. Somebody forgot to tear out the tracks and pull down the cables. So when it rains or snows some fool always gets caught and the slick tracks flip a car into a telephone pole or upside a hydrant and the cars just lay there with crumpled fenders and windshields shattered, laying there for no reason just like the tracks and wires are there for no reason now that buses run where the 88 and the 82 Lincoln trolleys used to go.

He remembers running down Lemington Hill because trolleys come only once an hour after midnight and he had heard the clatter of the 82 starting its long glide down Lincoln Avenue. The Dells still working out on *Why Do You Have to Go* and the tip of his dick wet and his balls aching and his finger sticky but he had forgotten all that and forgot the half hour in Sylvia's hallway because he was flying, all long strides and pumping arms and his fists opening and closing on the night air as he grappled for balance in a headlong rush down the steep hill. He had heard the trolley coming and wished he was a bird soaring through the black night, a bird with shiny chrome fenders and fishtails and a Continental kit. He tried to watch his feet, avoid the cracks and gulleys in the sidewalk. He heard the trolley's bell and crash of its steel wheels against the tracks. He had been all in Sylvia's drawers and she was wet as a dishrag and moaning her hot breath into his ear and the record player inside the door hiccuping for the thousandth time caught in the groove of gray noise at the end of the disc.

He remembers that night and curses again the empty trolley screaming past him as he had pulled up short half a block from the corner. Honky driver half sleep in his yellow bubble. As the trolley careened away red sparks had popped above its gimpy antenna. Chick had his nose open and his dick hard but he should have cooled it and split, been out her drawers and down the hill on time. He had fooled around too long. He had missed the trolley and mize well walk. He had to walk and in the darkness over his head the cables had swayed and sung long after the trolley disappeared.

He had to walk cause that's all there was to it. And still no ride of his own so he's still walking. Nothing to it. Either right or left, either up Homewood or down Homewood, walking his hip walk, making something out of the way he is walking since there is nothing else to do, no place to go so he makes something of the going, lets them see him moving in his own down way, his stylized walk which nobody could walk better even if they had some place to go.

Thinking of a chump shot on the nine ball which he blew and cost him a quarter for the game and his last dollar on a side bet. Of pulling on his checkered bells that morning and the black tank top. How the creases were dead and cherry pop or something on the front and a million wrinkles behind the knees and where his thighs came together. Junkie, wino-looking pants he would have rather died than wear just a few years before when he was one of the cleanest cats in Westinghouse High School. Sharp and leading the Commodores. Doo Wah Diddy, Wah Diddy Bop. Thirty-five-dollar pants when most the cats in the House couldn't spend that much for a suit. It was a bitch in the world. Stone bitch. Feeling like Mister Tooth Decay crawling all sweaty out of the gray sheets. Mom could wash them every day, they still be gray. Like his underclothes. Like every motherfucking thing they had and would ever have. Doo Wah Diddy. The rake jerked three or four times through his bush. Left there as decoration and weapon. You could fuck up a cat with those steel teeth. You could get the points sharp as needles. And draw it swift as Billy the Kid.

Thinking it be a bitch out here. Niggers write all over everything don't even know how to spell. Drawing power fists that look like a loaf of bread.

Thinking this whole Avenue is like somebody's mouth they let some jive dentist fuck with. All these old houses nothing but rotten teeth and these raggedy pits is where some been dug out or knocked out and ain't nothing left but stumps and snaggleteeth just waiting to go. Thinking, that's right. That's just what it is. Why it stinks around here and why ain't nothing but filth and germs and rot. And what that make me? What it make all these niggers? Thinking yes, yes, that's all it is.

Mr. Strayhorn where he always is down from the corner of Hamilton and Homewood sitting on a folding chair beside his iceball cart. A sweating canvas draped over the front of the cart to keep off the sun. Somebody said the old man a hundred years old, somebody said he was a bad dude in his day. A gambler like his own Granddaddy John French had been. They say Strayhorn whipped three cats half to death try to cheat him in the alley behind Dumferline. Took a knife off one and whipped all three with his bare hands. Just sits there all summer selling iceballs. Old and can hardly see. But nobody don't bother him even though he got his pockets full of change every evening.

Shit. One of the young boys will off him one night. Those kids was stone crazy. Kill you for a dime and think nothing of it. Shit. Rep don't mean a thing. They come at you in packs, like wild dogs. Couldn't tell those young boys nothing. He thought he had come up mean. Thought his running buddies be some terrible dudes. Shit. These kids coming up been into more stuff before they twelve than most grown men do they whole lives.

Hard out here. He stares into the dead storefronts. Sometimes they get in one of them. Take it over till they get run out or set it on fire or it gets so filled with shit and nigger piss don't nobody want to use it no more except for winos and junkies come in at night and could be sleeping on a bed of nails wouldn't make no nevermind to those cats. He peeks without stopping between the wooden slats where the glass used to be. Like he is reading the posters, like there might be something he needed to know on these rain-soaked, sun-faded pieces of cardboard talking about stuff that happened a long time ago.

Self-defense demonstration . . . Ahmed Jamal. Rummage Sale. Omega Boat Ride. The Dells. Madame Walker's Beauty Products.

A dead bird crushed dry and paper-thin in the alley between Albion and Tioga. Like somebody had smeared it with tar and mashed it between the pages of a giant book. If you hadn't seen it in the first place, still plump and bird colored, you'd never recognize it now. Looked now like the lost sole of somebody's shoe. He had watched it happen. Four or five days was all it took. On the third day he thought a cat had dragged it off. But when he passed the corner next afternoon he found the dark shape in the grass at the edge of the cobblestones. The head was gone and the yellow smear of beak but he recognized the rest. By then already looking like the raggedy sole somebody had walked off their shoe.

He was afraid of anything dead. He could look at something dead but no way was he going to touch it. Didn't matter, big or small, he wasn't about to put his hands near nothing dead. His daddy had whipped him when his mother said he sassed her and wouldn't take the dead rat out of the trap. He could whip him again but no way he was gon touch that thing. The dudes come back from Nam talking about puddles of guts and scraping parts of people into plastic bags. They talk about carrying their own bags so they could get stuffed in if they got wasted. Have to court-martial his ass. No way he be carrying no body bag. Felt funny now carrying out the big green bags you put your garbage in. Any kind of plastic sack and he's thinking of machine guns and dudes screaming and grabbing their bellies and rolling around like they do when they're hit on Iwo Jima and Tarawa or the Dirty Dozen or the Magnificent Seven or the High Plains Drifter, but the screaming is not in the darkness on a screen it is bright, green afternoon and Willie Thompson and them are on patrol. It is a street like Homewood. Quiet like Homewood this time of day and bombed out like Homewood is. Just pieces of buildings standing here and there and fire scars and places ripped and kicked down and cars stripped and dead at the curb. They are moving along in single file and their uniforms are hip and their walks are hip and they are kind of smiling and rubbing their weapons and cats passing a joint fat as a cigar down the line. You can almost hear music from where Porgy's Record Shop used to be, like the music so fine it's still there clinging to the boards, the broken glass on the floor, the shelves covered with roach shit and rat shit, a ghost of the music rifting sweet and mellow like the smell of home cooking as the patrol slips on past where Porgy's used to be. Then . . .

Rat Tat Tat . . . Rat Tat Tat . . . Ra Ta Ta Ta Ta Ta Ta . . .

Sudden but almost on the beat. Close enough to the beat so it seems the point man can't take it any longer, can't play this soldier game no longer and he gets happy and the smoke is gone clear to his head so he jumps out almost on the beat, wiggling his hips and throwing up his arms so he can get it all, go on and get down. Like he is exploding to the music. To the beat which pushes him out there all alone, doing it, and it is Rat Tat Tat and we all want to fingerpop behind his twitching hips and his arms flung out but he is screaming and down in the dirty street and the street is exploding all round him in little volcanoes of dust. And some of the others in the front of the patrol go down with him. No semblance of rhythm now, just stumbling, or airborne like their feet jerked out from under them. The whole hip procession buckling, shattered as lines of deadly force stitch up and down the Avenue.

Hey man, what's to it? Ain't nothing to it man you got it baby hey now where's it at you got it you got it ain't nothing to it something to it I wouldn't be out here in all this sun you looking good you into something go on man you got it all you know you the Man hey now that was a stone fox you know what I'm talking about you don't be creeping past me yeah nice going you got it all save some for me Mister Clean you seen Ruchell and them yeah you know how that shit is the cat walked right on by like he ain't seen nobody but you know how he is get a little something don't know nobody shit like I tried to tell the cat get straight nigger be yourself before you be by yourself you got a hard head man hard as stone but he ain't gon listen to me shit no can't nobody do nothing for the cat less he's ready to do for hisself Ruchell yeah man Ruchell and them come by here little while ago yeah baby you got it yeah lemme hold this little something I know you got it you the Man you got to have it lemme hold a little something till this evening I'll put you straight tonight man you know your man do you right I unnerstand yeah that's all that's to it nothing to it I'ma see you straight man yeah you fall on by the crib yeah we be into something tonight you fall on by.

Back to the left now. Up Hamilton, past the old man who seems to sleep beside his cart until you get close and then his yellow eyes under the straw hat brim follow you. Cut through the alley past the old grade school. Halfway up the hill the game has already started. You have been hearing the basketball patted against the concrete, the hollow thump of the ball glancing off the metal backboards. The ball players half naked out there under that hot sun, working harder than niggers ever did picking cotton. They shine. They glide and leap and fly at each other like their dark bodies are at the ends of invisible strings. This time of day the court is hot as fire. Burn through your shoes. Maybe that's why the niggers play like they do, running and jumping so much cause the ground's too hot to stand on. His brother used to play here all day. Up and down all day in the hot sun with the rest of the crazy ball players. Old dudes and young dudes and when people on the side waiting for winners they'd get to arguing and you could hear them bad-mouthing all the way up the hill and cross the tracks in the park. Wolfing like they ready to kill each other.

His oldest brother John came back here to play when he brought his family through in the summer. Here and Mellon and the courts beside the Projects in East Liberty. His brother one of the old dudes now. Still crazy about the game. He sees a dude lose his man and fire a jumper from the side. A double pump, a lean, and the ball arched so it kisses the board and drops through the iron. He could have played the game. Tall and loose. Hands bigger than his brother's. Could palm a ball when he was eleven. Looks at his long fingers. His long feet in raggedy ass sneakers that show the crusty knuckle of his little toe. The sidewalk sloped and split. Little plots of gravel and weeds where whole paving blocks torn away. Past the dry swimming pool. Just a big concrete hole now where people piss and throw bottles like you got two points for shooting them in. Dropping like a rusty spiderweb from tall metal poles, what's left of a backstop, and beyond the flaking mesh of the screen the dusty field and beyond that a jungle of sooty trees below the railroad tracks. They called it the Bums' Forest when they were kids and bombed the winos sleeping down there in the shade of the trees. If they walked alongside the track all the way to the park they'd have to cross the bridge over Home-wood Avenue. Hardly room for trains on the bridge so they always ran and some fool always yelling, *Train's coming* and everybody else yelling and then it's your chest all full and your heart pumping to keep up with the rest. Because the train couldn't kill everybody. It might get the last one, the slow one but it wouldn't run down all the crazy niggers screaming and hauling ass over Homewood Avenue. From the tracks you could look down on the winos curled up under a tree or sitting in a circle sipping from bottles wrapped in brown paper bags. At night they would have fires, hot as it was some summer nights you'd still see their fires from the bleachers while you watched the Legion baseball team kick butt.

From high up on the tracks you could bomb the forest. Stones hissed through the thick leaves. Once in a while a lucky shot shattered a bottle. Some gray, sorry-assed wino mother-fucker waking up and shaking his fist and cussing at you and some fool shouts *He's coming, he's coming*. And not taking the low path for a week because you think he was looking dead in your eyes, spitting blood and pointing at you and you will never go alone the low way along the path because he is behind every bush, gray and bloody-mouthed. The raggedy, gray clothes flapping like a bird and a bird's feathery, smothering funk covering you as he drags you into the bushes.

He had heard stories about the old days when the men used to hang out in the woods below the tracks. Gambling and drinking wine and telling lies and singing those old time, down home songs. Hang out there in the summer and when it got cold they'd loaf in the Bucket of Blood on the corner of Frankstown and Tioga. His granddaddy was in the stories. Old John French one of the baddest dudes ever walked these Homewood streets. Old, big-hat John French. They said his granddaddy could sing up a storm and now his jitterbug father up in the choir of Homewood A.M.E. Zion next to Mrs. Washington who hits those high notes. He was his father's son, people said. Singing all the time and running the streets like his daddy did till his daddy got too old and got saved. Tenor lead of the Commodores. Everybody saying the Commodores was the baddest group. If that cat hadn't fucked us over with the record we might have made the big time. Achmet backing us on the conga. Tito on the bongos. Tear up the park. Stone tear it up. Little kids and old folks all gone home and ain't nobody in the park but who supposed to be and you got your old lady on the side listening or maybe you singing pretty to pull some new fly bitch catch your eye in the crowd. It all comes down, comes together mellow and fine sometimes. The drums, the smoke, the sun going down and you out there flying and the Commodores steady taking care of business behind your lead.

"You got to go to church. I'm not asking I'm telling. Now you get those shoes shined and I don't want to hear another word out of you, young man." She is ironing his Sunday shirt hot and stiff. She hums along with the gospel songs on the radio. "Don't make me send you to your father." Who is in the bathroom for the half hour he takes doing whatever to get hisself together. Making everybody else late. Singing in there while he shaves. You don't want to be the next one after him. "You got five minutes, boy. Five minutes and your teeth better be clean and your hands and face shining." Gagging in the

funky bathroom, not wanting to take a breath. How you supposed to brush your teeth, the cat just shit in there? "You're
going to church this week and every week. This is my time
and don't you try to spoil it, boy. Don't you get no attitude
and try to spoil church for me." He is in the park now, sweating
in the heat, a man now, but he can hear his mother's voice
plain as day, filling up all the empty space around him just as
it did in the house on Finance Street. She'd talk them all to
church every Sunday. Use her voice like a club to beat everybody out the house.

His last time in church was a Thursday. They had up the
scaffolding to clean the ceiling and Deacon Barclay's truck was
parked outside. Barclay's Hauling, Cleaning and General Re-
pairing. Young People's Gospel Chorus had practice on Thursday and he knew Adelaide would be there. That chick looked
good even in them baggy choir robes. He had seen her on
Sunday because his Mom cried and asked him to go to church.
Because she knew he stole the money out her purse but he had
lied and said he didn't and she knew he was lying and feeling
guilty and knew he'd go to church to make up to her. Adelaide
up there with the Young People's Gospel Chorus rocking
church. Rocking church and he'd go right on up there, the lead
of the Commodores, and sing gospel with them if he could get
next to that fine Adelaide. So Thursday he left the poolroom,
*Where you tipping off to, Man? None of your motherfucking
business, motherfucker*, about seven when she had choir practice and look here, Adelaide, I been digging you for a long
time. Longer and deeper than you'll ever know. Let me tell
you something. I know what you're thinking, but don't say it,
don't break my heart by saying you heard I was a jive cat and
nothing to me and stay away from him he ain't no good and
stuff like that I know I got a rep that way but you grown enough
now to know how people talk and how you got to find things
out for yourself. Don't be putting me down till you let me have
a little chance to speak for myself. I ain't gon lie now. I been
out here in the world and into some jive tips. Yeah, I did my
time diddy bopping and trying my wheels out here in the street.
I was a devil. Got into everything I was big and bad enough
to try. Look here. I could write the book. Pimptime and par-
tytime and jive to stay alive, but I been through all that and
that ain't what I want. I want something special, something

166

solid. A woman, not no fingerpopping young girl got her nose open and her behind wagging all the time. That's right. That's right, I ain't talking nasty, I'm talking what I know. I'm talking truth tonight and listen here I been digging you all these years and waiting for you because all that Doo Wah Diddy ain't nothing, you hear, nothing to it. You grown now and I need just what you got. . . .

Thursday rapping in the vestibule with Adelaide was the last time in Homewood A.M.E. Zion Church. Had to be swift and clean. Swoop down like a hawk and get to her mind. Tuesday she still crying and gripping the elastic of her drawers and saying *No*. Next Thursday the only singing she doing is behind some bushes in the park. *Oh, Baby. Oh, Baby, it's so good*. Tore that pussy up.

Don't make no difference. No big thing. She's giving it to somebody else now. All that good stuff still shaking under her robe every second Sunday when the Young People's Gospel Chorus in the loft beside the pulpit. Old man Barclay like he guarding the church door asking me did I come around to help clean. "Mr. Barclay, I wish I could help but I'm working nights. Matter of fact I'm a little late now. I'm gon be here on my night off, though."

He knew I was lying. Old bald head dude standing there in his coveralls and holding a bucket of Lysol and a scrub brush. Worked all his life and got a piece of truck and a piece of house and still running around yes sirring and no mamming the white folks and cleaning their toilets. And he's doing better than most of these chumps. Knew I was lying but smiled his little smile cause he knows my mama and knows she's a good woman and knows Adelaide's grandmother and knows if I ain't here to clean he better guard the door with his soap and rags till I go on about my business.

Ruchell and them over on a bench. Niggers high already. They ain't hardly out there in the sun barbecuing their brains less they been into something already. Niggers be hugging the shade till evening less they been into something.

"Hey now."

"What's to it, Tom?"

"You cats been into something."

"You ain't just talking."

"Ruchell man, we got that business to take care of."

"Stone business, Bruh. I'm ready to T.C.B., my man."

"You ain't ready for nothing, nigger."

"Hey man, we're gon get it together. I'm ready, man. Ain't never been so ready. We gon score big, Brother Man . . ."

They have been walking an hour. The night is cooling. A strong wind has risen and a few pale stars are visible above the yellow pall of the city's lights. Ruchell is talking:

"The reason it's gon work is the white boy is greedy. He's so greedy he can't stand for the nigger to have something. Did you see Indovina's eyes when we told him we had copped a truckload of color tee vees. Shit man. I could hear his mind working. Calculating like. These niggers is dumb. I can rob these niggers. Click. Click. Clickedy. Rob the shit out of these dumb spooks. They been robbing us so long they think that's the way things supposed to be. They so greedy their hands get sweaty they see a nigger with something worth stealing."

"So he said he'd meet us at the car lot?"

"That's the deal. I told him we had two vans full."

"And Ricky said he'd let you use his van?"

"I already got the keys, man. I told you we were straight with Ricky. He ain't even in town till the weekend."

"I drive up then and you hide in the back?"

"Yeah dude. Just like we done said a hundred times. You go in the office to make the deal and you know how Indovina is. He gon send out his nigger Chubby to check the goods."

"And you jump Chubby?"

"Be on him like white on rice. Freeze that nigger till you get the money from Indovina."

"You sure Indovina ain't gon try and follow us?"

"Shit, man. He be happy to see us split . . ."

"With his money?"

"Indovina do whatever you say. Just wave your piece in his face a couple times. That fat ofay motherfucker ain't got no heart. Chubby his heart and Ruchell stone take care of Chubby."

"I still think Indovina might go to the cops."

"And say what? Say he trying to buy some hot tee vees and got ripped off? He ain't hardly saying that. He might just say he got robbed and try to collect insurance. He's slick like that. But if he goes to the cops you can believe he won't be describing us. Naw. The pigs know that greasy dago is a crook. Everybody knows it and won't be no problems. Just score and blow. Leave this motherfucking sorry ass town. Score and blow."

"When you ain't got nothing you get desperate. You don't care. I mean what you got to be worried about? Your life ain't shit. All you got is a high. Getting high and spending all your time hustling some money so you can get high again. You do anything. Nothing don't matter. You just take, take, take whatever you can get your hands on. Pretty soon nothing don't matter, John. You just got to get that high. And everybody around you the same way. Don't make no difference. You steal a little something. If you get away with it, you try it again. Then something bigger. You get holt to a piece. Other dudes carry a piece. Lots of dudes out there holding something. So you get it and start to carrying it. What's it matter? You ain't nowhere anyway. Ain't got nothing. Nothing to look forward to but a high. A man needs something. A little money in his pocket. I mean you see people around you and on TV and shit. Man, they got everything. Cars and clothes. They can do something for a woman. They got something. And you look at yourself in the mirror you're going nowhere. Not a penny in your pocket. Your own people disgusted with you. Begging around your family like a little kid or something. And jail and stealing money from your own mama. You get desperate. You do what you have to do."

The wind is up again that night. At the stoplight Tommy stares at the big sign on the Boulevard. A smiling Duquesne Pilsner Duke with his glass of beer. The time and temperature flash beneath the nobleman's uniformed chest. Ricky had installed a tape deck into the dash. A tangle of wires drooped from its guts, but the sound was good. One speaker for the cab, another for the back where Ruchell was sitting on the rolls of carpet Ricky had stacked there. Al Green singing *Call Me*. Ricky could do things. Made his own tapes; customizing the delivery van. Next summer Ricky driving to California. Fixing up the van so he could live in it. The dude was good with his hands. A mechanic in the war. Government paid for the wasted knee. Ricky said, Got me a new knee now. Got a four-wheeled knee that's gonna ride me away from all this mess. The disability money paid for the van and the customizing and the stereo tape deck. Ricky always have that limp but the cat getting hisself together.

Flags were strung across the entrance to the used car lot. The wind made them pop and dance. Rows and rows of cars looking clean and new under the lights. Tommy parked on the street, in the deep shadow at the far end of Indovina's glowing corner. He sees them through the office window. Indovina and his nigger.

"Hey, Chubby."

"What's happening now?" Chubby's shoulders wide as the door. Indovina's nigger all the way. Had his head laid back so far on his neck it's like he's looking at you through his noseholes instead of his eyes.

"You got the merchandise?" Indovina's fingers drum the desk.

"You got the money?"

"Ain't your money yet. I thought you said two vans full."

"Can't drive but one at a time. My partner's at a phone booth right now. Got the number here. You show me the bread and he'll bring the rest."

"I want to see them all before I give you a penny."

"Look, Mr. Indovina. This ain't no bullshit tip. We got the stuff, alright. Good stuff like I said. Sony portables. All the same . . . still in the boxes."

"Let's go look."

"I want to see some bread first."

"Give Chubby your keys. Chubby, check it out. Count em. Make sure the cartons ain't broke open."

"I want to see some bread."

"Bread. Bread. My cousin DeLuca runs a bakery. I don't deal with *bread*. I got money. See. That's money in my hand. Got plenty money buy your television sets buy your van buy you."

"Just trying to do square business, Mr. Indovina."

"Don't forget to check the cartons. Make sure they're sealed."

Somebody must be down. Ruchell or Chubby down. Tommy had heard two shots. He sees himself in the plate glass window. In a fishbowl and patches of light gliding past. Except where the floodlights are trained, the darkness outside is impenetrable. He cannot see past his image in the glass, past the rushes of light slicing through his body.

"Turn out the goddamn light."

"You kill me you be sorry...kill me you be real sorry ...if one of them dead out there it's just one nigger kill another nigger...you kill me you be sorry...you killing a white man..."

Tommy's knee skids on the desk and he slams the gun across the man's fat, sweating face with all the force of his lunge. He is scrambling over the desk, scattering paper and junk, looking down on Indovina's white shirt, his hairy arms folded over his head. He is thinking of the shots. Thinking that everything is wrong. The shots, the white man cringing on the floor behind the steel desk. Him atop the desk, his back exposed to anybody coming through the glass door.

Then he is running. Flying into the darkness. He is crouching so low he loses his balance and trips onto all fours. The gun leaps from his hand and skitters toward a wall of tires. He hears the pennants crackling. Hears a motor starting and Ruchell calling his name.

"What you mean you didn't get the money? I done wasted Chubby and you ain't got the money? Aw shit. Shit. Shit."

He had nearly tripped again over the man's body. Without knowing how he knew, he knew Chubby was dead. Dead as the sole of his shoe. He should stop; he should try to help. But the body was lifeless. He couldn't touch...

Ruchell is shuddering and crying. Tears glazing his eyes and he wonders if Ruchell can see where he's going, if Ruchell knows he is driving like a wild man on both sides of the street and weaving in and out the lines of traffic. Horns blare after them. Then it's Al Green up again. He didn't know how, when or who pushed the button but it was Al Green blasting in the cab. *Help me Help me Help me...*

Jesus is waiting... He snatches at the tape deck with both hands to turn it down or off or rip the goddamn cassette from the machine.

"Slow down, man. Slow down. You gonna get us stopped." Rolling down his window. The night air sharp in this face. The whir of tape dying then a hum of silence. The traffic sounds and city sounds pressing again into the cab.

171

"Nothing. Not a goddamn penny. Wasted the dude and we still ain't got nothing."

"They traced the car to Ricky. Ricky said he was out of town. Told them his van stolen when he was out of town. Claimed he didn't even know it gone till they came to his house. Ricky's cool. I know the cat's mad, but he's cool. Indovina trying to hang us. He saying it was a stickup. Saying Chubby tried to run for help and Ruchell shot him down. His story don't make no sense when you get down to it, but ain't nobody gon to listen to us."

"Then you're going to keep running?"

"Ain't no other way. Try to get to the coast. Ruchell knows a guy there can get us IDs. We was going there anyway. With our stake. We was gon get jobs and try to get it together. Make a real try. We just needed a little bread to get us started. I don't know why it had to happen the way it did. Ruchell said Chubby tried to go for bad. Said Chubby had a piece down in his pants and Ruchell told him to cool it told the cat don't be no hero and had his gun on him and everything but Chubby had to be a hard head, had to be John Wayne or some goddamned body. Just called Ruchell a punk and said no punk had the heart to pull the trigger on him. And Ruchell, Ruchell don't play, brother John. Ruchell blew him away when Chubby reached for his piece."

"You don't think you can prove your story?"

"I don't know, man. What Indovina is saying don't make no sense, but I heard the cops ain't found Chubby's gun. If they could just find that gun. But Indovina, he a slick old honky. That gun's at the bottom of the Allegheny River if he found it. They found mine. With my prints all over it. Naw. Can't take the chance. It's Murder One even though I didn't shoot nobody. That's long, hard time if they believe Indovina. I can't take the chance...."

"Be careful, Tommy. You're a fugitive. Cops out here think they're Wyatt Earp and Marshall Dillon. They shoot first and maybe ask questions later. They still play wild, wild West out here."

"I hear you. But I'd rather take my chance that way. Rather they carry me back in a box than go back to prison. It's hard out there, Brother. Real hard. I'm happy you got out. One of us got out anyway."

"Think about it. Take your time. You can stay here as long as you need to. There's plenty of room."

"We gotta go. See Ruchell's cousin in Denver. Get us a little stake then make our run."

"I'll give you what I can if that's what you have to do. But sleep on it. Let's talk again in the morning."

"It's good to see you, man. And the kids and your old lady. At least we had this one evening. Being on the run can drive you crazy."

"Everybody was happy to see you. I knew you'd come. You've been heavy on my mind since yesterday. I wrote a kind of letter to you then. I knew you'd come. But get some sleep now. . . . we'll talk in the morning."

"Listen, man. I'm sorry, man. I'm really sorry I had to come here like this. You sure Judy ain't mad?"

"I'm telling you it's OK. She's as glad to see you as I am. . . . And you can stay . . . both of us want you to stay."

"Running can drive you crazy. From the time I wake in the morning till I go to bed at night, all I can think about is getting away. My head ain't been right since it happened."

"When's the last time you talked to anybody at home?"

"It's been a couple weeks. They probably watching people back there. Might even be watching you. That's why I can't stay. Got to keep moving till we get to the coast. I'm sorry, man. I mean nobody was supposed to die. It was easy. We thought we had a perfect plan. Thieves robbing thieves. Just score and blow like Ruchell said. It was our chance and we had to take it. But nobody was supposed to get hurt. I'd be dead now if it was me Chubby pulled on. I couldna just looked in his face and blown him away. But Ruchell don't play. And everybody at home. I know how they must feel. It was all over TV and the papers. Had our names and where we lived and everything. Goddamn mug shots in the Post Gazette. Looking like two gorillas. I know it's hurting people. In a way I wish it had been me. Maybe it would have been better. I don't really care what happens to me now. Just wish there be some way to get the burden off Mama and everybody. Be easier if I was dead."

"Nobody wants you dead. . . . That's what Mom's most afraid of. Afraid of you coming home in a box."

"I ain't going back to prison. They have to kill me before I go back in prison. Hey, man. Ain't nothing to my crazy talk.

173

You don't want to hear this jive. I'm tired, man. I ain't never been so tired.... I'ma sleep...talk in the morning, Big Brother."

He feels his brother squeeze then relax the grip on his shoulder. He has seen his brother cry once before. Doesn't want to see it again. Too many faces in his brother's face. Starting with their mother and going back and going sideways and all of Homewood there if he looked long enough. Not just faces but streets and stories and rooms and songs.

Tommy listens to the steps. He can hear faintly the squeak of a bed upstairs. Then nothing. Ruchell asleep in another part of the house. Ruchell spent the evening with the kids, playing with their toys. The cat won't ever grow up. Still into the Durango Kid, and Whip Wilson and Audie Murphy wasting Japs and shit. Still Saturday afternoon at the Bellmawr Show and he is lining up the plastic cowboys against the plastic Indians and boom-booming them down with the kids on the playroom floor. And dressing up the Lone Ranger doll with the mask and guns and cinching the saddle on Silver. Toys like they didn't make when we were coming up. And Christmas morning and so much stuff piled up they'd be crying with exhaustion and bad nerves before half the stuff unwrapped. Christmas morning and they never really went to sleep. Looking out the black windows all night for reindeer and shit. Cheating. Worried that all the gifts will turn to ashes if they get caught cheating, but needing to know, to see if reindeer really can fly.

SOLITARY

To reach the other world you changed buses twice. The first bus took you downtown and there you caught another to the Northside. Through the Golden Triangle, across the Sixth Street Bridge, the second bus shuttled you to Reed Street on the Northside where you waited for one of the infrequent expresses running out Allegheny River Boulevard to the prison. With perfect connections the trip might take an hour and three quarters each way but usually a whole day was consumed getting there and getting back with the visit to her son sandwiched between eternities of waiting. Because the prison was in another world. She hadn't understood that at first. She had carried with her into the prison her everyday expectations of people, her sense of right and wrong and fairness. But none of that fit. The prison mocked her beliefs. Her trips to see her son were not so much a matter of covering a certain distance as they were of learning the hostile nature of the space separating her from him, learning how close and how far away he would always be. In the time it took to blink, the time it took for a steel gate to slam shut behind her, he would be gone again, a million miles away again and the other world, gray and concrete, would spring up around her, locking him away as abruptly as the prison walls.

One Sunday, walking the mile from the prison gate to the unsheltered concrete island which served as a bus stop and shivering there for over an hour in freezing November rain she had realized the hardships connected with the visits to her son were not accidental. The trips were supposed to speak to her plainly. Somebody had arranged it that way. An evil somebody who didn't miss a trick. They said to reach him you must suffer, you must fight the heat and cold, you must sit alone and be beaten by your thoughts, you must forget who you are and be prepared to surrender your dignity just as you surrender your purse to the guard caged outside the waiting room entrance. In the prison world, the world you must die a little to enter, the man you've traveled so far to see is not your son but a number. He is P3694 and you must sit on a hard, wooden bench in a filthy waiting room until that number is called. Then it's through steel doors and iron bars and buzzing machines which peek under your clothes. Up stairs and down stairs and across a cobbled corridor dark and chill even in summer and you are inside then and nothing you have brought from the outside counts. Not your name, your pain, your love. To enter you must be prepared to leave everything behind and be prepared when you begin the journey home to lose everything again.

That is the trip she must take to see him. Not hours and buses but a brutal unraveling of herself. On the way back she must put herself together again, compose herself, pretend the place she has been doesn't exist, that what surrounds her as the bus lumbers along the Boulevard is familiar and real, that the shopping center and factories and warehouses crowding the flanks of Allegheny River Boulevard served some useful, sane purpose and weren't just set out to taunt her, to mock her helplessness. Slowly she'd talk herself into believing again. This bus will take me to Reed. Another will cross the bridge into town. I'll catch the 88 and it will shudder over the Parkway and drop me five blocks from home. And when I am home again I will be able to sit down in the brown chair and drink a cup of coffee and nod at some foolishness on TV, and nothing I do, none of these little lies which help me home again will hurt him or deny him. Because he is in another world, a world behind stone walls higher than God's mercy.

Sometimes she says that to herself, says the prison is a place her God has forsaken. But if He is not there, if His Grace does not touch her son then she too is dwelling in the shadow of unlove. If she can make the journey to the Valley of the Shadow, surely He could penetrate the stone walls and make His presence known. She needs weeks sometimes to marshall her strength for the trip. She knows what it costs her: the sleepless nights, the rage and helplessness, the utter trembling exhaustion bracketing the journey. How she must fight back tears when she sees his face, hears his voice. How guilt and anger alternate as she avoids people's faces and shrinks into a corner of a bus. She prays the strangers won't see her secrets, won't laugh at her shame, won't shatter in the icy waves of hatred pouring from her frozen heart. She knows her blood pressure will soar sky high and the spasms of dizziness, of nausea will nearly knock her off her feet. She needed weeks to prepare for all of that and weeks of recovering before she gathered strength enough to begin planning another trip, but she rode the buses and walked the miles and waited the eternities. Surely the walls weren't too tall, too thick for Him. He could come as a cloud, as a cleansing wind.

The prison was built close to the river. She wondered if the men could see it from their cells. She had meant to ask Tommy. And if her son could see it, would the river flowing past make him feel better or feel worse. In spring the sloping bank beyond the iron fence of the visitors' parking lot turned green. The green wasn't fair, didn't make sense when she noticed it for the first time as she stopped in the asphalt and gravel margin between the prison's outer wall and the ten-foot-tall iron fence along the river. A border of green edging the brown river which didn't make sense either as she stopped to blow her nose. For a moment as she paused and stared across the water everything was absolutely still. A wad of tissue was balled in her fist, the river glided brownly, silently past but nothing else was real. Everything so still and quiet she believed that she had fallen out of time, that she had slipped into an empty place between worlds, a place unknown, undreamed of till that moment, a tiny crack between two worlds that was somehow in its emptiness and stillness vaster than both.

The green was sectioned by the iron spears of the fence. Between the sharp points of the spears clusters of spikes riveted to the top railing of the fence glittered in the sun. The sky was blue, the river brown, the grass green. The breeze off the water whispered spring and promised summer but God let his sunshine play in the crowns of needle-pointed spikes. Near the top of the wall she could make out a row of windows deeply recessed, darker than the soot-grimed stones. If Tommy was standing at one of the screened windows could he see the river, the green, the gray pit into which she had slipped?

A coal barge hooted. She stuffed her tissue back in her purse. She thought she could hear the men's voices echoing from behind the walls, voices far away in a cave, or deep inside a tunnel, a jumbled, indistinct murmur out of which one voice would eerily rise and seem to mutter inches from her ear. If she could, she would have run from the yard. The voices hated her. They screamed obscenities and made fun of everything about her. She didn't have the strength to run but wouldn't have run if she could because that would only give them more to laugh at, would bring them howling and nipping at her heels as she fled to the bus stop.

From the visitors' entrance to the bus stop was a walk of nearly a mile. A nameless street paralleled one black prison wall, then crossed a flat, barren stretch of nothing before it intersected Allegheny River Boulevard. From the bus stop she looked back at the emptiness surrounding the prison. The dark walls loomed abrupt and stark. Like the green river bank the walls had no reason to be there, nothing connected them to the dusty plain of concrete. The walls were just there, like the lid of a roasting pan some giant hand had clamped down. It made no sense but it was there and no one could move it, no one was trying to disturb the squat black shape even though her son was dying beneath it.

This is the church and this is the steeple. Open the doors and out come the people. She let her hands form what she was thinking. Her wiggling fingers were ants scrambling for a wedge of daylight.

Her God had razed the proud walls of Jericho with nothing more than screaming horns. She let her hands fall to her sides and closed her eyes, but the walls were still there when she looked again.

On the first of the buses back to Homewood she tried to think of what she'd say to the others. What she would tell them when they asked, How is he? Should she say he's a million miles away? That his name is different in the other world? That he is heavier, thicker in the shoulders, but the baggy prison clothes hang loosely on his body so he seems like a little boy? Should she say his bitterness toward her is mellowing? Or does his anger hurt her less now only because she has listened so many times to his accusations? He says he has relived every single moment of his life. He turns the days over and over, asking questions, reconstructing incidents, deciding what he should have done, analyzing what he did do and what others did to him. In the story of his life which he dreams over and over again, she comes up a villain. Her love, her fears are to blame. She held the reins too tightly or she let him run loose; she drowned him in guilt with her constant questions, her tears at his slightest trespass or she didn't ever really pay enough attention to him. His hurting words would tear her down. She'd stop trying to defend herself, grow numb. His voice would fade from her consciousness and her mind would wander to a quieter, safer place. She'd daydream and free herself from the choking web of his bitterness. She'd want to ask him why he thought she made these wearying journeys. Did he think she came to be whipped? Did he think he had a right to take out his frustrations on her just because she was the only one who'd listen, who'd travel the million miles to where he was caged? But she wouldn't ask those questions. She'd listen till she drifted to that leaden, numb place where nothing could touch her. If someone to scream at was what he needed, she'd be that someone.

She wouldn't tell them anything like that when they asked, How is he? At the bus stop on Reed street she rehearsed what she would say, what she always said, *Better. He's doing better. It's a hateful place but he's doing better.* Corrugated tin sheeting and transparent plastic panels formed a back and slanting half-roof partially enclosing the platform. Like standing in a seashell when the roar of traffic buffeted her. This morning only an occasional car rumbled by. All over town they were ripping up the old trolley tracks and asphalting their cobblestone beds but at this end of Reed street anything that moved rattled against the cobbles like it was coming apart. She was alone till a boy crossing from the far side of the street joined her on the platform. His transistor radio was big as a suitcase and his music vibrated the shelter's tin roof. He was skinny like Tommy had been. A string bean, bean pole like her son Tommy and like him this one pranced when he walked and danced to the music while he was standing still.

Tommy was *Salim* now. She had told them his new name but she had no words for what had happened to his eyes, his cheekbones, the deepening shadows in his face. To herself she'd say his eyes burned, that his flesh was on fire, that the bones of his face were not hard and white, but something kindling beneath his skin, that the fire burned with sharp knife edges and his skin hung on the points of flame and the dark hollows of his face were where the fire shone blackly through his brown skin. His eyes screamed at her. It hurt him to be what he was, where he was, but he had no words for it either. Only the constant smoldering of his flesh, the screaming of his eyes.

"He's stronger much stronger. The Muslim business and the new name scare me but it's something for him to hold on to. They have their own little group. It gives him a chance to be somebody. He has his bad days of course. Especially now that the weather's getting nice. He has his bad days but he's made up his mind that he's going to stay on top of it. He's going to survive."

She'd say that. She'd answer with those words each time one of them asked about him. She'd say the words again and again till she was certain she believed them, till she was certain the words were real.

He'd been in the Behavior Modification Unit six weeks now. Six weeks out of the six months of solitary confinement they'd slapped on him. They called it the B.M.U., the Hole. To her it was a prison within a prison. Something worse happening after she thought she'd faced the worst. Twenty-three hours a day locked in his cell. Forty-five minutes of exercise in the yard if a guard was free to supervise him. If not, tough. Twenty-four hours alone in a ten by eight box. One meal at eleven, the other at two. *If you could call them meals, Mom.* Nothing till the next eleven o'clock meal except coffee and a hunk of bread when he was awakened. Two meals in three hours and no food for the next twenty-one. A prison within a prison. A way of telling him and telling her never to relax, never to complain because things could always get worse.

Instead of staying on the last bus till it reached her stop she got off at Frankstown and Homewood. They had both stood when the visiting room guard called his number. Tommy had wrapped his arms around her and hugged her, drawn her as close as he could to the fires alive inside him. Then he had turned from her quickly, striding across the scarred floor toward the steel gate from which he had entered. He hadn't turned back to look at her. The smell of him, the warmth, the strength of his arms circling her so suddenly had taken her breath away. She had wanted to see his face again, had almost cried out at those shoulders which were a man's now, which sloped to his arms and long, dangling hands and tight round butt and gangly legs with his bare ankles hanging down out of the high water prison pants. She had believed nothing could hurt more than the bottled-up anger he spewed at her but she had been wrong. The hug hurt more. His arms loving her hurt more. And when he turned like a soldier on his heel and marched away from her, eyes front, punishing the floor in stiff, arm rigid strides she was more alone than she had ever been while he raged.

So she stepped off the bus at Frankstown and Homewood because she didn't want to be alone, didn't want to close her front door behind her and hear the bolts and chains clicking home in the stillness, and didn't want to greet the emptiness which would rush at her face, pelt it like the dusty, littered wind when it raced across the barren plain outside the prison walls.

This was his street, Tommy's stomping ground. One hot summer night they'd burned it. Looted and burned Homewood Avenue so the block between Hamilton and Kelley was a wasteland of vacant lots and blackened stone foundations and ramshackle wooden barricades guarding the craters where stores and shops had once done business. This was the same Homewood Avenue her Daddy had walked. Taller than the buildings in his high-crowned, limp-brimmed hat. Big-hat John French strutting like he owned Homewood and on his good nights he probably did, yes, if all the stories she had heard about him were true, he probably did own it. Her father, her sons, the man she married, all of them had walked up and down Homewood Avenue so she got off before her stop because she didn't want to be alone. They'd walk beside her. She could window-shop in Murphy's 5&10, listen to the music pouring from the open door of the Brass Rail and Porgy's Record Shop, look

183

DAMBALLAH

at the technicolored pictures advertising coming attractions at
the Bellmawr Show. She could hear it and see it all, and walk
in the company of her men even though the storefronts were
boarded or demolished altogether or transformed to unfamiliar,
dirty-looking shops and her men were gone, gone, gone.

On the far corner of Homewood and Kelley the brick and
stone Homewood A.M.E. Zion church stood sturdy and solid
as a rock. She almost crossed over to it. Almost climbed the
cement steps and pushed through the red door. She knew she'd
find silence there and knew at the foot of the purple-carpeted
aisle she could drop to her knees in a familiar place and her
God would listen. That if she left her pride in the ravaged street
and abandoned her hate and put off her questions He would
take her to His bosom. He would bathe her in the fount of His
Grace and understand and say well done. She almost stepped
off the broken curb and ran to His embrace but the stolid church
they had purchased when white people started running away
from Homewood didn't belong on the Avenue this afternoon.
She stared at it like she'd stared at the prison and the green
river bank. He had to have a plan. For her life or anybody's
life to make sense He had to have a plan. She believed that
and believed the plan would reveal His goodness but this long
day she could only see gaps and holes, the way things didn't
connect or make sense.

Now she knows she is walking to the park. Homewood
Avenue with its ghosts and memories was not what had drawn
her off the bus early. Homewood Avenue was just a way to
get somewhere and clearly now she understood she was walking
toward the park.

She turned left at Hamilton, the street where the trolleys
used to run. Then past the library where the name of her great
uncle Elmer Hollinger was stamped on the blackened bronze
plaque with the rest of the Homewood veterans of World War
I. The family went back that far. And farther when you listened
to May and Gert tell about the days when bears and wildcats
lived in Homewood and Great-great-grandfather Charley Bell
was the one first chopped down a tree here. Past the library
then across Hamilton and up the hill alongside old Homewood
school. The building in which she had started first grade was
still standing. Tinny looking outcroppings and temporary sheds
hid most of the old walls but her grade school was still standing.

Somewhere she had a picture of her third grade class posed on the front steps, between the thick columns which supported the porch of old Homewood school. More white faces than black in those days, and long aproned dresses, and stiff collars and she is a pale spot at the end of one row, couldn't tell she was colored unless you looked real close and maybe not even then. No one was smiling but she remembered those days as happy, as easy, days she quickly forgot so each morning was like starting life all over again, new and fresh. Past the school yard where they're always playing basketball, past the pool the city stopped filling years ago so now it's just a huge garbage can you can smell from blocks away in the summer. At the top of the hill a footbridge to the park crosses the railroad tracks. They say the little house below the bridge on a platform built out from the park side of the tracks was where the trains stopped for George Westinghouse. His private station, and any train his people signaled knew it better stop for him. He was like a king they said. Owned half of Pittsburgh. The park belonged to him. The two white buildings where the maintenance men keep their tools and tractor were once a stable and a cottage for his servants. It was Westinghouse Park because the great man had donated it to the city. Kids had broken all the windows in the little house. For as long as she could remember it had been an empty shell, blind and gutted, a dead thing beside the tracks.

From the footbridge she could look down on the shape of the park, the gravel paths dividing it into sections, the deep hollow running along Albion Street, the swings and slides in a patch of brown over near the tracks, the stone benches, the whitewashed buildings at the far end. In spite of huge trees blocking her view she saw the park in detail. She had been coming to Westinghouse Park since she was a baby so she could see it with her eyes closed.

From the bridge the grass seemed a uniform green, a soft unbroken carpet the way it is in her dreams when she comes with her mother and her sisters and brother to sit on the steep sides of the hollow. On summer Sundays they'd wear white and spread blankets on the grass and watch the kids whooping like wild Indians up and down the slope, across the brown floor of the hollow their feet had rubbed bare. She had wondered why her mother dressed them in white then dared them to come

185

home with one spot of dirt on their clothes. She had envied the other children romping and rolling down the sides of the hollow. Sunday is the day of rest her mother would say, God's peace day so she'd dress them in white and they'd trudge up Tioga Street to the park with rolled blankets tucked under their arms. Her mother would read the magazines from the Sunday paper, watch the grown-ups promenade along the paths, and keep track of every breath her children drew. *Mama got eyes like a hawk*, her brother would whisper. *Eyes in the back of her head*. Sooner or later he'd escape just long enough to get grass stains on his knee or backside, just long enough for his sisters to see a white streak flashing in the whirl of dark bodies down in the hollow. Then she'd get mad at her brother Carl and join her voice with her mother's summoning him back. *Running with that pack of heathens like he ain't got good sense*. Sometimes her bones ached to tumble and somersault down the green slope, but there were moments, moments afloat with her sisters on the calm, white clouds of their dresses, when she knew nothing could be better than the quiet they shared far away from anyone, each in her own private corner of the bluest sky.

She calls her brother from the open door of the Brass Rail. *Carl, Carl*. Her voice is lost in the swirl of music and talk animating the darkness. The stale odor of beer and pee and disinfectant blocks the entrance. Her brother Carl is at the far end of the bar talking to the barmaid. He is hunched forward, elbows on the chrome rail, his long legs rooted in the darkness at the base of his stool. He doesn't hear her when she calls again. The stink rolling in waves from the open door of the men's room works on her stomach, she remembers she's eaten nothing since coffee in the morning. She starts when a voice just inside the door shouts her brother's name.

"Carl. Hey Carl. Look here, man."

Her brother turns toward the door and frowns and recognizes her and smiles and begins to dismount his stool all at once.

"Hey Babe. I'm coming." He looks more like their daddy every day. Tall like him, and bald on top like John French, even moving like their father. A big man's gentle, rolling shuffle. A man who walked softly because most things had sense enough to get out of his way. A large man gliding surely but slowly, like John French once did through the streets of

Homewood because he wanted to give the benefit of the doubt to those things that couldn't move quite so quickly as others out of his path.

"Could you walk with me a minute? Walk with me up to the park?"

"Sure, Babe. Sure I'll walk with you."

Did he sound like John French? Was his voice getting closer to their father's? She remembers words John French had said. She could hear him laugh or hear his terrible coughing from the living room that year he sat dying in his favorite chair. Those noises were part of her, always would be, but somehow she'd lost the sound of her father's speaking voice. If Carl was getting more like him every day maybe she'd learn her father's voice again.

"I've just been to see Tommy."

"No need to tell me that. All I had to do was look at your eyes and I knew where you'd been."

"It's too much. Sometime I just can't take it. I feel like I'd rather die than make that trip."

"You try and relax now. We'll just walk a little bit now. Tommy knows how to take care of hisself in there and you got to learn how to take care of yourself out here. Did you take your medicine today?"

"Yes. I swallowed those hateful pills with my coffee this morning for all the good they do."

"You know how sick you get when you don't take em. Those pills are keeping you alive."

"What kind of life is it? What's it worth? I was almost to the park. I got as far as the bridge and had to turn around and come back. I wanted to walk over there and sit down and get my nerves together but I stopped halfway across the bridge and couldn't take another step. What's happening to me, Carl? I just stood there trembling and couldn't take another step."

"It's hard. It's hard out here in the world. I know that and you know that, it's hard and cold out here."

"I'm no child. I'm not supposed to break down and go to pieces like I did. I'm a grown woman with grown children. I walked all the way from Frankstown just to go to the park and get myself together but I couldn't get across that silly bridge. I need to know what's happening to me. I need to know why."

"Let's just walk. It's nice in the park this time of day. We

187

can find us a bench and sit down. You know it'll be better in the park. Mama'll keep her hawk eyes on us once we get to the park."

"I think I'm losing Him."

"Something happen in there today? What'd they do to Tommy?"

"Not Tommy. Not Tommy this time. It's God I'm losing. It's Him in me that's slipping away. It happened in the middle of the bridge. I was looking down and looking over into the park. I was thinking about all those times I'd been to Westinghouse Park before. So much on my mind it wasn't really like thinking. More like being on fire all over your body and rushing around trying to beat down the flames in a hundred places at once and doing nothing but making it worse. Then I couldn't take another step. I saw Mama the way she got after her stroke, the way she was when she stopped talking and walking after Daddy died. You remember the evil look she turned on anybody when they mentioned church or praying. I saw her crippled the way she was in that chair and I couldn't take another step. I knew why she cursed Him and put God out of her life when she started talking again. I knew if I took another step I'd be like her."

She feels Carl's arm go around her shoulder. He is patting her. His big hips get in the way and bump her and she wants to cry out. She could feel the crack begin at the top of her forehead, hear it splitting and zigzagging down the middle of her body. Not his hard hip bone that hurt. She was a sheet of ice splintering at the first touch.

"I'd lose Him if I took another step. I understood Mama for the first time. Knew why she stopped walking and talking."

"Well, I'm here now. And we're gon cross now to the park. You and me gon sit down under those big pretty trees. The oldest trees in Homewood they say. You musta heard May tell the story about the tree and the bear and Great-great-granddaddy Bell killing him with a pocket knife. That woman can lie. You get her riding a bottle of Wild Turkey and she can lie all night. Keep you rolling till your insides hurt."

"Mama was right. She was right, Carl."

"Course she was. Mama was always right."

"But I don't want to be alone like she was at the end."

"Mama wasn't never alone. Me and Gerry were there under

188

the same roof every morning she woke up. And you and Sissy visited all the time. Mama always had somebody to do for her and somebody she could fuss at."

She hears her brother's words but can't make sense of them. She wonders if words ever make sense. She wonders how she learned to use them, trust them. Far down the tracks, just beyond the point where the steel rails disintegrated into a bright, shimmering cloud on the horizon line she sees the dark shape of a train. Just a speck at this distance. A speck and a faint roar rising above the constant murmur of the city. She had never liked standing on the skimpy bridge with a train thundering under her feet. Caught like that on the bridge she wouldn't know whether to run across or leap under the churning wheels.

Her God rode thunder and lightning. He could be in that speck the size of a bullet hurtling down the tracks. If you laid your ear on the track the way Carl had taught her you could hear trains long before you'd ever see them. In a funny way the trains were always there, always coming or going in the trembling rails so it was really a matter of waiting, of testing then waiting for what would always come. The black bullet would slam into her. Would tear her apart. He could strike you dead in the twinkling of an eye. He killed with thunder and lightning.

She stopped again. Made Carl stop with her in the middle of the bridge, at the place she had halted before. She'd wait this time, hold her ground this time. She'd watch it grow larger and larger and not look away, not shut her ears or stop her heart. She'd wait there on the shuddering bridge and see.

THE BEGINNING OF HOMEWOOD

I have just finished reading a story which began as a letter to you. A letter I began writing on a Greek island two years ago, but never finished, never sent, a letter which became part of the story I haven't finished either. Rereading makes it very clear that something is wrong with the story. I understand now that part of what's wrong is the fact that I never finished the letter to you. The letter remains inside the story, buried, bleeding through when I read. What's wrong is the fact that I never finished the letter, never sent it and it is buried now in a place only I can see. Because the letter was meant for you. I began by trying to say some things to you, but they never got sent, never reached you so there is something wrong about the story nothing can fix.

In a way the story came before the letter. The story concerned the beginning of Homewood and a woman, a black woman who in 1859 was approximately eighteen years old. She was the property of a prosperous farmer who employed slave labor to cultivate the land he owned near Cumberland, Maryland. I wanted to tell the story of the woman's escape, her five-hundred-mile flight through hostile, dangerous territory and her final resettlement in Homewood, a happy ending or beginning from our point of view since this woman turns out to be Great-great-great-grandmother Sybela Owens. The idea of the story had been on my mind for years, ever since I'd heard Aunt May tell it the night of Grandpa's funeral. For some reason being in Europe again sharpened the need to get it down on paper. Maybe the trip to the concentration camp at Dachau, maybe the legend I'd heard about Delos, an island sacred to Apollo where no one was allowed to be born or to die, maybe the meals alone in restaurants where no one else was speaking English, maybe the Greek word *helidone* which means swallows and sounds like a perfect poem about birds, maybe all of that had something to do with sharpening the need. Anyway I was sitting in a cafe scribbling messages on postcards. Halfway through the stack I got tired of trying to be cute and funny and realized the only person I needed to write was you. So I started a letter in my notebook. And that's when the first words of Sybela Owens's story said themselves. Five or six sentences addressed to you and then the story took over.

Aunt May's voice got me started on the story. Sitting in a cafe, staring out at the gray sky and gray sea, and mad because it was my last morning on the island and I'd been hoping for blue skies and sunshine, sitting there trying to figure out why I was on a Greek island and why you were six thousand miles away in prison and what all that meant and what I could say to you about it, I heard Aunt May's voice. She was singing Lord reach down and touch me. I heard the old church rocking through the cries of sea birds. *Lord, reach down and touch me*, the Gospel Chorus of Homewood African Methodist Episcopal Zion Church singing, *Touch me with Thy holy grace* because *Lord if you would touch me, Thy touch would save me from sin*. And Aunt May was right there singing with them. You know how she is. Trying to outsing everybody when the congregation harmonizes with the Gospel Chorus. She had on one of those funny square little hats like she wears with all the flowers and a veil. I could hear her singing and I could feel her getting ready to shout. In a minute she'd be up and out in the aisle shaking everything on her old bones she could shake, carrying on till the ushers came and steadied her and helped her back to her seat. I could see the little hat she keeps centered just right on top of her head no matter how hard the spirit shakes her. And see her eyes rolling to the ceiling, that yellow ceiling sanctified by the sweat of Deacon Barclay and the Men's Auxiliary when they put up the scaffolds and climb with buckets of Lysol and water and hearts pumping each year a little less strongly up there in the thin air to scrub the grit from the plaster so it shines like a window to let God's light in and let the prayers of the Saints out.

That's when the story, or meditation I had wanted to decorate with the trappings of a story began. At least the simple part of it. The part concerning the runaway and her dash for freedom, the story I had been trying to tell for years. Its theme was to be the urge for freedom, the resolve of the runaway to live free or die. An old, simple story, but because the heroine was Great-great-great-grandmother Sybela Owens, I felt the need to tell it again.

What was not simple was the crime of this female runaway set against your crime. What was not simple was my need to tell Sybela's story so it connected with yours. One was root and the other branch but I was too close to you and she was too far away and there was the matter of guilt, of responsibility. I couldn't tell either story without implicating myself.

This woman, this Sybela Owens our ancestor, bore the surname of her first owner and the Christian name, Sybela, which was probably a corruption of Sybil, a priestess pledged to Apollo. The Sybil of Greek myth could see the future but her power was also a curse because like the black woman tagged with her name centuries later, Sybil was a prisoner. A jealous magician had transformed the Greek Sybil into a bird, caged her and robbed her of speech. She possessed only a song and became a bauble, a plaything in a gilded cage set out to entertain dinner guests in the wizard's palace. This was to be her role for eternity, except that once, addressed by a seer who heard a hauntingly human expressiveness in her song, she managed to reply, "My name is Sybil and I wish to die."

On the plantation Sybela Owens was called Belle. Called that by some because it was customary for slaves to disregard the cumbersome, ironic names bestowed by whites, and rechristen one another in a secret, second language, a language whose forms and words gave substance to the captives' need to see themselves as human beings. Called Belle by others

195

because it was convenient and the woman answered to it. Called Belle by a few because these older slaves remembered another black woman, an African who had lived with a cage on her shoulders for twenty years and the cage had a little tinkling bell attached to it so you knew when she was coming and naturally they had started calling her Bell, in derision at first, mocking her pride, her futile stubbornness on a point most of the women had conceded long before, a point which peopled the plantation with babies as various in hue as the many colors of Joseph's coat, then Belle because she had not broken, Mother Belle finally because she was martyr and saint, walking among them with the horrible contraption on her shoulders but unwavering, straight and tall as the day the iron cage had been fitted to her body; her pride their pride, her resistance a reminder not of the other women's fall, but of the shame of those who had undone them. Called Belle because they saw in this beautiful Sybela a striking resemblance, a reincarnation almost of the queenly, untouchable one who had been sent to suffer with them.

Every morning the slaves were awakened by the blast of a conch shell. Blowing the conch horn would have been a black man's job. To be up before everybody else while the sky was still dark and the grass chilly with dew. A black man would have to do it. And do it to the others who hated to hear him as much as he hated the cold walk in his bare feet to the little rise where he was expected to be every morning and every morning like he was some kind of goddamn rooster stand there and blast away on the conch till other feet started shuffling in the rows of dark huts.

Sybela would have heard the conch shell a thousand mornings. Strangely, the first morning of her freedom when she heard nothing but bird cries and the rasp of crickets, she missed the horn. The three or four dresses in which she had cocooned herself unfurl as she rolls away from Charlie Bell's hard back. She shivers as a draft runs up between her clothes and her skin, breaking the seal of heat. She stares at the horizon while the sky drifts grayly across the mirror of her eyes. In the rifts between the dark hills, mist smolders dense and white as drifted snow; the absolute stillness is stiller and more absolute because of the ground noise of birds and insects. She rises to a sitting position and lifts her arm from the rags beneath which her

196

children sleep and hugs the mantle of her entire wardrobe closer to her body. In the quiet moments of that first morning of freedom she misses the moaning horn and hates the white man, her lover, her liberator, her children's father sleeping beside her.

Charlie Bell had stolen her, her and the two children, stolen them from his own father when he learned the old man intended to include them in a lot of slaves sold to a speculator. She had no warning. Just his knock, impatient, preemptive as it always was when he decided to take her from her sleep. Using no more words than he did when he demanded her body, he made it clear what he wanted. In a few minutes all that was useful and portable was gleaned from the hut, the children roused, every piece of clothing layered on their backs and then all of them rushing into the night, into the woods bordering the northern end of the plantation. He pushed them without words, a rage in his grunts, in his hands, rage she felt aimed at her and the frightened children though it was the forest he tore at and cursed. The dark woods responded to his attack with one of their own: branches whipped at the runaways' faces, roots snarled their feet, dry wood snapped loud enough to wake the dead.

It began, like most things between them, in silence, at night. After an hour or so they had to carry the children. Charlie Bell lifted Maggie who was older and heavier than her brother, and Sybela draped Thomas in the sling across her chest not because she conceded anything to the man's strength but because when she bowed into the darkness she reached for the sobs of fear and exhaustion she knew the man could not quiet. Maggie would cling to Charlie Bell, the plunge through the forest would become a game as she burrowed her head into his shoulder. She would be riding a horse and the jostling gallop, the fury of the man's heartbeat would lull her to sleep. But the boy was frightened more by the white man than the crashing forest. Thomas was not much more than a baby but he would scramble along on his thin, bowlegs till he dropped. Never complaining, Thomas would pick himself up a hundred times and not even notice the shrieks of invisible animals, but he could not abide the man's presence, the man's anger, and he whined until Sybela pressed him to sleep against her body.

The first morning of her freedom she looked quickly away

from the white man, forgetting the knife-thrust of hatred as she listened to the complaints of her body and surveyed the place where exhaustion had forced them to drop. Charlie Bell must know where they are going. She had heard stories of runaways traveling for weeks in a great circle that brought them back to the very spot where they had begun their escape. The man must know. All white men seemed to know the magic that connected the plantation to the rest of the world, a world which for her was no more than a handful of words she had heard others use. The words *New Orleans, Canada, Philadelphia, Cumberland* were impossible for her to say. Except silently to herself, sifting them through her mind the way old heathen Orion was always fingering the filthy string of beads he wore around his neck. She did not hear the conch shell and realized for the first time in her life she was alone. In spite of the children still tied to her with strings that twisted deep inside her belly, in spite of the man, she knew she could just walk away from all of them, walk away even if the price was heavy drops of her blood dripping at every step because she was nowhere and no one was watching and the earth could swallow her or the gray sky press down like a gigantic pillow and snuff out her life, her breath, the way Charlie Bell had tried once, and it would be nobody but her dead, nobody knowing her death just like nobody heard in the silence of this morning her thoughts; and that was the thing she would not walk away from, the drone of her voice speaking to itself, monotonous and everlasting as cricket hum. She could not leave it, or bury it and cry over it; she was nothing but that sound, and the sound was alone.

I wanted to dwell on Sybela's first free morning but the chant of the Gospel Chorus wouldn't let me sit still. *Lord, reach down and touch me.* The chorus wailing and then Reba Love Jackson soloing. I heard May singing and heard Mother Bess telling what she remembers and what she had heard about Sybela Owens. I was thinking the way Aunt May talks. I heard her laughter, her amens, and *can I get a witness*, her digressions within digressions, the webs she spins and brushes away with her hands. Her stories exist because of their parts and each part is a story worth telling, worth examining to find the stories it contains. What seems to ramble begins to cohere when the listener understands the process, understands that the voice seeks to recover everything, that the voice proclaims *nothing is lost*, that the listener is not passive but lives like everything else within the story. Somebody shouts *Tell the truth*. You shout too. May is preaching and dances out between the shiny, butt-rubbed, wooden pews doing what she's been doing since the first morning somebody said *Freedom*. Freedom.

One of the last times I saw you, you were in chains. Not like Isaac Hayes when he mounts the stage for a concert or poses for an album cover, not those flaunted, ironic, who's-shucking-who gold chains draped over his ten-thousand-dollar-a-night brown body but the real thing, old-time leg irons and wrist shackles and twenty pounds of iron dragged through the marbled corridors of the county courthouse in Fort Collins, the Colorado town where they'd finally caught up with you and your cut buddy Ruchell. I waited outside the courtroom for a glimpse of you, for a chance to catch your eye and raise my clenched fist high enough for you and everybody else to see. I heard a detective say: "These are a couple of mean ones. Spades from back East. Bad dudes. Wanted in Pennsylvania for Murder One."

You and Ruchell were shackled together. In your striped prison issue coveralls you were the stars everyone had been awaiting. People murmured and pointed and stared and the sea of faces parted for your passage. In the eyes of the other green-coveralled prisoners waiting to be arraigned there was a particular attentiveness and awe, a humility almost as they came face to face with you—the Big Time. Your hair was nappy and shot straight out of the tops of your heads. Made you look a foot taller. Leg irons forced you to shuffle; your upper bodies swayed to make up for the drag of the iron. Neither of you had shaved. Neither looked down at the gaggle of deputies shooing back the crowd. The two of you could have been a million miles away discussing Coltrane or pussy. Everything about your faces disclaimed the accident that was happening to your bodies. The slept-in, too small coveralls, the steel bracelets, the rattling pimp-strut shuffle through the marbled hallway some other black prisoner had freshly mopped. You were intent on one another, smiling, nodding, whispering inside a glass cage. I thought of your ambition to be an entertainer. Admired the performance you were giving them.

Bad dudes. Mean nigger men. Killers.

If they had captured Great-great-great-grandmother Sybela

Owens, they would have made a spectacle of her return to the plantation, just as they paraded you, costumed, fettered through the halls. Because they had not allowed you soap or combs or mirrors or razors, you looked as if you had been hiding for days in the bush, bringing some of its wildness with you into the clean halls of justice. She too, if they had caught her, would have returned part wild thing. Her long hair matted, her nails ragged and caked with mud, her skirts in tatters, the raw smell of the woods soaked into her clothes and skin. She would have struggled to walk unbowed behind the horses, at the end of the rope depending from her wrists to saddle horn. Her eyes would have been fixed in the middle distance, beyond the slumped backs of the sleepy riders, above the broken line of slave row cabins the hunting party finally reached. Her shoes would be gone, her wrists bloody. There would be dark splotches across her back where the coarse homespun cloth has fused with her flesh. The shame she will never speak of, more bearable now than it will ever be because now it is a fiery pain in her groin blotting out the humiliation she will remember and have to deal with once the pain has subsided. A funky, dirty black woman, caught and humbled, marched through the slave quarters like the prize of war she is, like the pawn she is in the grand scheme of the knights on horseback. But her eyes are on the moon. Like yours. I ask myself again *why not me*, why is it the two of you skewered and displayed like she would have been if she hadn't kept running. Ask myself if I would have committed the crime of running away or if I would have stayed and tried to make the best of a hopeless situation. Ask if you really had any choice, if anything had changed in the years between her crime and yours. Could you have run away without committing a crime? Were there names other than "outlaw" to call you, were there words other than "crime" to define your choice?

Mother Bess is down off Bruston Hill now. She talks about you and asks about you and says God give her strength she's crossing that river and coming over to see you. She talks about Sybela Owens. May saw Sybela Owens too. May was staring at the tall, straight trees behind the house when she felt eyes on her, eyes which had burrowed right down into the place where she was daydreaming. May let her own eyes slowly find the ones watching her. Cautiously she lowered her gaze down past the tall trees, the slant of the roof, the rhythmed silhouette of gray shingles and boards, down past the scarred post supporting the porch roof, the knobby uprights of the rocking chair's back, stopping finally at the old woman who sat dark and closed as a fist. Sybela Owens's ancient eyes blinked in the bright sunlight but did not waver; they had waited patiently as if they had all the time in the world for May to reach them. Then it was May's turn to wait. She quieted everything inside herself as the old eyes shushed her and patted her and said her name in a way she had never heard it said before. *May.* The eyes never left her, but after an instant which seemed forever, May was released. Sybela Owens's eyes never left her but they had fallen asleep again. Among the million brown wrinkles and folds in the old woman's face were two invisible shutters which slid down over her eyes. They were in place again and though May could not see through them, she understood that Grandmother Owens could still look out.

"And let me tell you all something. That's right. You all listen up because I'm gon tell you what you ain't never heard. That's right. And you heard it from May and May be long gone but you all remember where you heard it. Yes indeed. About Grandmother Owens now. She had power. A freeing kind of power. I heard them say it and you might hear somebody say it and think that's just old people talking or them old time down home tales don't nobody believe no more but you listen to me and hear me tell it like it was because I was there, me, May, and I wasn't nothing but a child in knickers but I had sense enough to know it when I felt it, sense enough to let the power touch me, yes Lawd, reach down and touch me, and I felt it from my nappy head down to my dirty toes, felt it even though I was a child, felt it raising me up from scratching at my backside and playing in dirt. Grandmother Owens touched me and I felt it. Felt all the life running out me and something new filling me up at the same time. Just as clear as a bell I heard her say my name. And say so many other things there ain't no words for but they all rushing in so fast felt my whole self moving out the way to make room. Thought her power gon bust me wide open. Bust me clean open and I be running down off that hill like melting snow."

And Mother Bess said, Tell the truth. Said, Yes. Yes. And May kept on telling.

"That's all. Ain't no more. Old as she was and young as I was, she let me feel the power. And I'm a witness. That's what I am now. Your Aunt May's a witness. I'm telling you it happened and I don't know much else about Grandmother Owens except what I been told cause that's the only time I seen her. Just before they brought her down off Bruston Hill. Didn't last a month they say. Took her down off that hill and she was dead in a month, a month after they carried her down. Strong enough to fight when they came for her. But she let them take her. Know she let them cause if she set her mind on not moving, nobody on God's green earth could budge that woman a inch. Because she had the power. I'm a witness. Had it still as sure as she sitting in that rocking chair in petticoats and a black cape and a long black dress. Sun hot as fire and she never sweat one bit. Had it and touched me with it. And changed my life. Yes she did. Told me to live free all this time and be a witness all this time. And told me come a day her generations fill this city and need to know the truth.

"Yes, Lawd. Everybody talking about heaven ain't going there. Hmmph. And everybody talking about freedom ain't been free and never gon be. If the Lord set a burden on you so heavy you can't move nothing but one thumb, you better believe what I'm telling you, the wiggling of that one thumb make you the freest thing in the world. Grandmother Owens now. She suffered in Egypt. She suffered under them cruel pharaohs. Told her when to jump and when to spit and beat her unmerciful she didn't jump or spit fast enough to suit em. That's what it was all about. Evil pharaohs and Hebrews who was God's chosen people, chosen to suffer and get hard like iron in a fire. Now youall see people just like I do, see them every day strutting round here in them fancy clothes or riding them big cars and they don't know they's still jumping and spitting when they told. They don't know it. Too ignorant to know it. Hmmph. And tell you *g'wan out my face, nigger*, you try and tell them something. But it be the same. Pharaohs and Hebrew children. Cept some few like Grandmother Owens get up one morning and gone. Run a hundred miles a day with little children on her back, her and that white man Charlie Bell and them babies run by night and sleep by day, crisscrossing rivers and forests full of alligators and wolves. Now that's something, ain't it? Grandmother Owens wasn't hardly no more than a child. Hardly old as Shirley sitting there but she got up one bright morning and heard the freedom trumpet and lit out not knowing a thing but she was gon keep running till she free. . . ."

On the first night of her first day of freedom after the children had finally fallen asleep under her arm and Charlie Bell's restless tossing had quieted to the grunting and twitching of a hound dog dreaming of a hunt, and the stars and insects reigned absolute in the darkness, Sybela thought she saw a star fall and remembered the old story about a night when all of heaven had seemed to come unstuck and hundreds of stars plummeted from the sky and you couldn't hear the rooster or the conch horn next morning for the prayers rising from the cabins. Niggers took the fiery night for a sign of Judgment Day coming. And the story said didn't nobody go to work that morning and didn't none the white folks come round and say a mumbling word neither. She believed she saw the star go, let go like a leaf does a tree, then tumble not like a leaf but with a stone's dead heaviness through water. But the dark waters of the sky closed up without a ripple so she couldn't be sure whether she saw a star fall or not. The swift turning of her eye loosed one of the tears brimming there and it slanted coolly and hotly down her cheek and she didn't know its source any more than she understood why one star tumbled and the other didn't and after she dug the back of her hand into both eyepits and her eyes were bone dry again she couldn't be sure if there had been a tear any more than she could be sure the flicker of motion crossing a corner of her eye had been an actual star's dying.

"They some the first settle here in Homewood. On Hamilton Avenue where Albion comes in. Trolley cars used to be on Hamilton but Charlie and Sybela Owens come here long before that. Most the city still be what you call Northside now. Old Allegheny then. Wasn't but a few families this side the river and hardly none at all out this way when Grandmother Owens come. Brought two children from slavery and had eighteen more that lived after they got here. Most born up on Bruston Hill after the other white men let Charlie know they didn't want one of their kind living with no black woman so Charlie he up and moved. Way up on Bruston Hill where nobody round trying to mind his business. Stead of killing them busybodies he took Grandmother Owens up there and that's the start of Homewood.

203

Children and grandchildren coming down off that hill and settling. Then other Negroes and every other kind of people moving here because the life was good and everybody welcome.
They say the land Charlie owned on Hamilton was fixed. After
he left, nothing grow or prosper there. They say Grandmother
Owens cursed it and Charlie warned all them white folks not
to touch his land. He said he would go to keep peace but
nobody better not set a foot on the land he left behind. That
spiteful piece of property been the downfall of so many I done
forgot half the troubles come to people try to live there. You
all remember where that crazy woman lived what strangled her
babies and slit her own throat and where they built that fancy
Jehovah Witness church over on Hamilton that burnt to the
ground. That's the land. Lot's still empty cept for ashes and
black stones and that's where Grandmother Owens first lived.
What goes round comes round, yes it does, now."

And Mother Bess said Preach. Said Tell the truth.

Sybela's story could end here but it doesn't. I still hear
May's voice:

"It hurts me. Hurts me to my heart. I remembers the babies.
How beautiful they were. Then somebody tells me this one's
dead, or that one's dying or Rashad going to court today or
they gave Tommy Life. And I remembers the babies. Holding
them. Seeing them once or twice a year at somebody's wedding, somebody's funeral or maybe at the Westinghouse picnic.
Sitting on a bench at Kennywood Park watching the merry-go-
round and listening to the music and a brown-skinned boy walk
by with his arm around a little gal's shoulder and he grin at
me all sheepish or turn his head real quick like he don't know
the funny looking old lady on the bench, and I know he's one
of the babies and remember the last time I saw him and how
I patted his nappy head and said *My, my, you sure are getting
big* or *My, my, you're grown now, a big man now*, and remember him peeking at me with the same sheepish grin and
don't you know that's what I remembers when I hear he's
robbed a store or been sent to prison or run off from some girl
he's left with a baby, or comes around on Westinghouse picnic
day at Kennywood Park to ask me for some ride money or to
show me his family, his babies and let .ne hold them a minute."

My story could end here, now. Sybela Owens is long dead,
rocking on the porch in her black cape like the sea taxis on

their anchors when the water is too mean for the journey to Delos. Great-great-great-grandmother Owens is meeting May's eyes, gazing through the child to the shadowy generations, to storms which will tilt the earth on its axis. The old woman watches her children fall like stars from the night sky, each one perfect, each one a billion years in the making, each one dug from her womb so the black heavens are crisscrossed infinitely by the filaments of her bright pain which no matter how thinly stretched are unbreakable and connect her with her progeny and each point of light to every other. The vision blinds her. She sighs and crosses her wrists under the ruins of her bosom.

It could end here or there but I have one more thing to tell you. The Supreme Court has decided to hear a case in which a group of inmates are arguing that they had a right to attempt an escape from prison because conditions in the prison constituted cruel and unusual punishment and thereby violated the prisoners' human rights. It's a bitch, ain't it? The Court has a chance to say yes, a chance to author its version of the Emancipation Proclamation. The Court could set your crime against Sybela's, the price of our freedom against yours. The Court could ask why you are where you are, and why the rest of us are here.

So the struggle doesn't ever end. Her story, your story, the connections. But now the story, or pieces of story are inside this letter and it's addressed to you and I'll send it and that seems better than the way it was before. For now. Hold on.

About the Author

John Edgar Wideman went to school in Pittsburgh and to the universities of Pennsylvania and Iowa. He was a Rhodes scholar at Oxford, was Professor of English at the University of Wyoming, and now teaches at the University of Massachusetts at Amherst. His nonfiction work, *Brothers and Keepers*, was selected as one of the ten best books of 1984 by the editors of *The New York Times Book Review*. The other two books in the Homewood Trilogy, *Hiding Place* and *Sent for You Yesterday* (winner of the prestigious PEN/Faulkner Award for Fiction), are also available in Vintage.